To Dorothy,

with best wishes

GHOST MOON

By the same author

GHOST MOON

Ron Butlin

CROMER

PUBLISHED BY SALT

12 Norwich Road, Cromer, Norfolk NR27 0AX United Kingdom

Printed in Great Britain by Clays Ltd, St Ives plc

Typeset in Sabon 10/13

ISBN 978 1 907773 77 8 paperback

1 3 5 7 9 8 6 4 2

To my wife, Regi, my sister Pam and my mother Elizabeth

PART ONE

SUNDAY

THE BLIZZARD WAS full-on – three hours instead of one with freezing fog, black ice and snow-snow-snow all the way. Penicuik, the Devil's Beef Tub, then tailgating the same Argos lorry over the Moffat Hills, snailing it behind Mr and Mrs Cautious down the M74.

A one-man avalanche from Edinburgh – you've made it. You're here. That's what counts.

And so . . .

Time to get psyched up, get focused.

But first things first—

Log on. You've been driving for ever, so there's bound to be something. So many messages, so many puffs of oxygen to keep you breathing. It's not just you, of course – you can see it in people's faces when their mobiles ring, the relief that somebody wants them.

C U @ 8 lol J x

The lovely Janice. You text her, confirming . . . and that's you back on solid ground. Another Sunday, another Mum visit, then a seventies download and the body-contour leather to carry you safely home. Second shave, second shower and into the second-best suit – for Janice, plus all the trimmings.

Takes care of the day, takes care of you.

Your phone snapped shut, you breathe easy once more.

Life's good.

Well, isn't it?

Zap-lock the car.

The path's needing shovelled clear and salted. A good six inches' worth. Fuck. If only you'd thought to bring your magic wand! But no probs. Fifteen minutes tops will see it —

No.

No. No.

The front door's locked and her key's still in the mortice, inside. Jesus. How often have you told her about that key, about not leaving it in the lock? Maybe she's not been out all weekend? Maybe she's fallen? Can't get herself out of the bath?

Which'll mean breaking down the door.

Not again.

A good loud knock first, loud enough to wake the —

No. Don't even think of it.

Thumping your fist big time. The snow's running ice-wet under your collar, the wind's razor-cutting your face. *Stamp-stamp-stamping* your feet on the front step to stop them turning into blocks of ice. You spoke on the phone only a few hours ago. She'd sounded fine, looking forward to seeing you.

You're freezing. *Stamp-stamp-stamp. Thump-thump-thump* . . .

Ninety years lying crumpled in a heap on the living room floor like she's —

Don't even think —

Thank God.

The time it's taking her to turn the key in the lock . . .

'Yes?' Her tone of voice, like she's never met you before.

Not opening the door enough to let you in.

'Mum? It's Sunday. I've come to—'

'Your *mother*? Are you sure you've got the right house? I'm Mrs Stewart. Maggie Stewart.'

'Let me in, Mum. I'm freezing out here. It's me. Tom.'

'Tom? You know Tom?' Her face suddenly all smiles. Opening the door a little more. 'You've some news of him?'

'News? It's *me*, I'm telling you.'

'But you do *know* Tom?'

'Of course I know—'

'Then you'd better come in.'

At last. Into the cottage, into her sitting room – and a coal fire blazing in the grate. That's more like it.

'Well then, and how *is* Tom?' She sits down.

'But, Mum, can't you see it's me?'

'I was told he'd be well looked after, so I hope he's fine. Mrs Saunders was most reassuring.'

'Mrs Saunders? Who's Mrs—?'

'Tom won't remember her, of course. He was far too young. Between you and me, it's best he never hears her name. Best for everyone.'

What the hell's she on about? The melted snow's dripping into your eyes, down your neck, your back. You want a towel. You want a seat. You want to get warmed up.

'Don't you recognise me, Mum? Today's Sunday. I've driven down from Edinburgh same as always to see you—'

Noticing you've glanced across at the tea trolley beside her, laid out with the usual straggled columns of playing cards—

'Learned to play patience during the war, and still keep it up,' she tells you. Like you didn't know already. 'Learned how to cheat then, too. The way you cheated turned into new rules so the game could go on. It had to, so you'd survive.'

Like she's talking to a complete stranger.

'Played it while waiting for the bombs to fall, sitting there in the black-out, waiting and waiting. Hearing the planes, the anti-aircraft guns in Leith . . .'

Best to move things along. 'I'll make us some tea.'

Through to the kitchen. Water. Kettle. A towel for the hair.

Tea in the pot. Mugs, milk jug, plate of biscuits. Finish off the drying, set up the tray. Then through to get the afternoon back on course.

'Here we are, Mum. I found a packet of HobNobs.'

Getting everything back to a normal Sunday. Some tea, some talk. Fix what needs fixed. Clear her path, then hit the road in time to begin the arctic crawl that'll take—

But . . . her photos? What's she done with the signed publicity shot of you as Mr Magic? It should be on the mantelpiece. And the lace curtains? What's she taken them down for? Might make the room seem brighter, but—

'. . . if the game worked out. We got bombed anyway. I was the only one in the family to survive. Nowhere to stay till the laird in the big house took pity. Lived here ever since. Sixty years and more, would you believe?'

Talking like you'd never lived here yourself, weren't brought up here. Like she's never seen you before. Doesn't even *know* you.

Can it happen that sudden?

She's half-rising from her chair as if to greet you for the first time. Such a warm, warm smile – you've not seen the like for months. So unexpected, so different from how she usually—

'You needn't worry, I'm really pleased to see you. I really am. I always knew you'd come.' She's almost in tears. Happy tears.

'But I always do, Mum! I come every Sunday, don't I? When we spoke this morning I—'

'I *knew* you'd come.' She's taken your hand and begun drawing it slowly down her face so your fingertips rest briefly on her eyes, her cheeks. Her lips.

What the hell's all this?

'I'm so very, very happy.'

Next thing, she's led you across to the window where you stand side by side gazing out at her garden and the countryside beyond, a complete white-out of fields, woods and sky as far as you can see. Now the snow's easing off there's a few patches of faint blue, a last handful of tumbling flakes.

Gripping your arm: '*That's* how I knew.' Pointing to what at first looks like a smudged fingerprint on the glass, a daytime moon: 'Everything'll be fine now, won't it, now you're here?'

And next moment she's touching *your* face, *your* eyes, cheeks, lips. She smiles again, 'And you *are* here, aren't you?' She's so happy, happier than you've seen her in a very long time.

Quite unexpectedly, she steps up close and kisses you on the mouth.

'Mum?'

At the same moment she's put her arms round you, pressing herself against you: 'I'm so pleased, so—'

'Stop, Mum! What're you doing?' You pull away from her. 'No. No. You can't—'

'Michael! Michael, please—'

Michael? Your father? She thinks that you're—?

You take a step back. As gently as possible, holding her at arms' length.

'It's me, Mum. Tom. It's Sunday, same as always, and I've come to see you.' Does she understand what you're saying? 'Mum? Don't you know who I—?'

The utter desperation in her face now, the wretchedness.

Then her anger, sudden and out of nowhere: 'Yes, I know who *you* are. I know all about you.'

Her anger, then utter fury.

'Get out of my house!' Screaming now, almost losing her balance as she staggers a couple of steps. 'Get out! Get out!' Her arm waving wildly towards the door. 'OUT!'

You can see what's going to happen next. About to fall, she's clutched at the trolley . . .

Which tips over, scattering playing cards everywhere . . .

You rush over and manage to catch her just in time.

Saving the day.

Nice one. That's you – a safe pair of hands. *Mr Magic*, right enough. Forget the no-kids and marriage number three flushed down the pan with no regrets, you're all she's got. She knows it, too. Deep down. She must do. She loves you.

And it's only a moment later – when you're helping your mother back to her seat, your arm holding her and keeping her steady – that she turns and spits in your face.

I

Listen, Maggie: as the years continue to slip from your grasp, you can see your younger self in front of you – thirty-year-old Maggie Davies as was, walking the length of the ship and back again, alone, past oil drums and coils of rusted chain, past the covered lifeboat creaking on its ropes.

No one else on deck, not a breath of wind, and the June sun failing to break through the half-mist, half-drizzle cloud that hangs above the dull heaviness of sea.

Up and down, up and down the wet boards, she goes . . .

Apart from the muffled *chug-chug-chug* of the ship's engine somewhere below, the only sounds are from seagulls screeching overhead and the propellers churning up the sullen stillness of the Minch. Maggie is glad of her woollen beret, her gabardine and scarf – these are all the outdoor clothes she's brought. The trip is not a holiday.

Lying here in the near-darkness of your bedroom in the care home, adrift between past and present, you're being carried to and fro by currents that run deeper than any measured time, currents that crisscross days, years and decades alike. *Your* days and years – until once again you're on that small ferry sailing from Mallaig to Stornoway. The salt-sea dampness in the air washes over you, the smell of paraffin almost turning your stomach whenever you pass too near the stern . . .

How clearly it's all coming back to you now, more vivid than any long-ago photograph could ever be. Mumble-singing to yourself: 'Speed bonnie boat, like a bird on the wing . . .'

Straining to open your eyes, desperate for the reassurance of the familiar chest of drawers, the wardrobe and easy chair you've brought with you from your cottage to Rosehaven House, your toiletries arranged on the glass shelf above the wash hand basin, the tea trolley with its half-finished game of patience waiting for you, the portable DAB radio beside your bed . . .

Sixty years foreshortened at a glance – like when you'd stood at your living-room window that morning, gazing out across the countryside under snow . . . yesterday, was it? Last week? Last month? No matter. Overnight, a handful of precious stones had been scattered across the pane where they'd frozen solid – an arrested cascade of light. Too cold to go out, the side roads probably blocked, and the pearl-sheen sky hard as a sheet of ice. The path up to the big house would be impossible for walking. Across on Keir's Hill, you could see some of the village children stumbling about in the snow, trying to clear a run for their sledges—

That's when you saw it, high above the village, and remembered the name you'd made up all those years ago.

A ghost moon.

So comforting it seemed to you then, as you'd paused for a moment at your cottage window, and so familiar. You traced its outline, hardly daring to press your fingertip on the chill glass, afraid the sliver of unexpected light might melt to nothing at your touch.

But there's no need to be afraid any more, Maggie, and no need to pretend. When the past returns, it is already an act of pretence. There's no shame in this – for how else could anyone bear to go on living?

Close your eyes and watch as Maggie Davies continues to pace the wooden deck. See, she's come to a sudden stop to stare down into the cold waters of the Outer Hebrides. A solitary woman, a mere silhouette pressed by chance against a backdrop of mist and sunless water . . .

The bedsheet feels slightly tight across your chest where it's been tucked in. They wanted you to be comfortable is all, and feel secure. The worst is over, Maggie, and the best just about to begin. Really.

Though it's still daylight outside, the woman you call Boss Beryl has already been in to draw your curtains. She pulled the door shut behind her when she left, without a word.

Close your eyes. Something wonderful is about to happen. Listen—

W HEN THE FERRY docked in Stornoway, Maggie struggled down the swaying wooden gangway, her heavy suitcase
bumping against her legs. No Waverley Station this with its
grime and grit, no soot-blackened walls and layers of soiled
daylight seeping down through the trapped, filthy air – the
ship's arrival had been perfectly timed for her to see the mist
being burned away to reveal a Hebridean sky so vast, so gen-
erous and light-filled it looked newly made. There was the
clean smell of sea and of heaped cod, mackerel and salmon
packed in ice – the morning's catch being winched ashore to
be stacked on the quayside next to the creels of live lobster
and crab. But as for the stench of gutted fish wafting in the
hot sun – she had to move further away, and quickly.

The white-bricked harbour master's office was so spick-
and-span it must surely have been built only the day before,
ready to greet her. Two men who might have been father and
son were lifting fish boxes into a van. Seagulls celebrated her
safe arrival by strutting up and down the quayside, screeching
in excitement, and rising into the air every few seconds only
to settle again a yard or so nearer to the dripping crates. The
older man looked up and addressed her in Gaelic. Maggie
shook her head.

'Grand day, missus!' His unfamiliar cadence, its singsong
gentleness, made the commonplace greeting sound like an
ancient psalm of welcome.

'Really beautiful!' She smiled back at him.

What energy surged through her! What hope! Coming here had cost her more than she could afford, but what choice had she? Nowhere to stay in Edinburgh, no job and her small savings soon to run out. Nobody knew her here, not really. The Isle of Lewis was a foreign country near enough, a new beginning surely.

By the time she'd found out what bus she should take, it had already departed and the next wasn't due to leave until the following morning.

A taxi?

She'd no money for taxis.

But then she'd no money for hotels either.

The boarding house Maggie was directed to overlooked Stornoway harbour. The landlady, a woman who introduced herself as Mrs Stewart, ushered her into the sitting room, talking all the while about the promise of a good summer to come and asking if she'd be taking a cup of tea with them?

'This is my son Michael,' she added, indicating a man in his thirties seated by the fire.

Maggie was surprised when son Michael made no move to get up from his chair to greet her; instead he simply held out his hand, letting it waver slightly as he fumbled the empty air to make contact.

'Pleased to meet you.' His voice had such unexpected warmth and assurance that she let her hand remain in his as he invited her to lean towards him. Next moment, he had reached up to pass his fingers over her face. It only took a few seconds, his fingertips were so gentle she hardly felt their touch. His eyes meanwhile remained still, seeming to be permanently awash with milk. She kept expecting him to blink to clear his vision, but he never did.

While she and Mrs Stewart discussed terms, Maggie noticed that the glass on the mantelpiece clock had been removed. Hours later, lying sleeplessly upstairs, she was to imagine the blind man getting up from his chair, taking a few steps across the well-charted darkness to hold his hands up to the clock face in front of him, feeling for the time.

The cost of one night's lodging settled, she was shown up to the first-floor bedroom. Having pointed out the bathroom and WC at the end of the corridor, the older woman then lowered her voice to explain about her son returning from the war, blinded for life. 'But at least he came back. Not like my husband.' Adding, as if to remind herself: 'We count ourselves lucky.'

Dinner was fish and chips, sitting on a bench that overlooked the sea. Then Maggie took a walk round the harbour before returning to the boarding house. It was still light when she went to bed.

'A grand summer's morning, sure enough. On holiday, are you?' Mrs Stewart had come through to offer more tea.

'Just a short break.'

'That'll be nice – a few days to yourself before your husband joins you.'

Though her porridge hadn't had time to cool properly, Maggie at once doubled her spooning rate. 'I've never been to Lewis before and hear it's beautiful.'

'Aye, when the rain's crossed to the mainland and the

midges are safe in their beds, it has a beauty like nowhere else on earth. You could try visiting the west coast, over Bernera way.'

'Well . . .'

'You'll have folk to visit, more like?' The teapot was positioned on its protective cork mat, the tea-cosy replaced.

Hot spoonful after hot spoonful was being cleared rapidly under Mrs Stewart's steady gaze.

'Can I get you some toast, Mrs Davies?'

'No thank you, Mrs Stewart. I'd best be getting my things ready.' One last spoonful and she was finished. 'Thank you for the lovely breakfast – a great start to the day.' She got to her feet. 'I'll look in before I go, to settle up.'

Ten minutes later Maggie made her way to the terminus where the bus waited to take her to the Eye Peninsula.

Once out of Stornoway, the Portnaguran bus rattled and bumped along the single track road sounding its horn every few minutes to warn slow-moving horse-and-carts to pull into the nearest passing place. It stopped to let off passengers at small villages, at road ends and junctions, at single houses even. When it crossed the open stretch of causeway the bus seemed to fill with light and, on either side, there was a glitter of sun-splashed waters and endless sky. The peninsula itself was flat moorland, utterly treeless. Maggie began keeping watch for road signs announcing the next huddle of cottages and the occasional black house with its turf roof – the village of Knock . . . then Melbost . . . Sleebost . . .

The photograph showed a stone-built house set well back from the road. The Callanders were distant family. Maggie had never met them, but for as long as she could remember there'd been an exchange of Christmas cards between the two households. On taking over their croft a year or so before, they'd written to her parents inviting them to visit any time, adding that their daughter, if she was still living at home, might fancy coming over for a longer stay. She could help around the croft and with the peat-cutting, they'd suggested – and there were more than enough local men back from the war who were still looking for a wife! 'Maybe you'd have better luck in the Hebrides than in these awful dance halls,' her mother had remarked as she'd propped up the photograph on the mantelpiece, next to some postcards. *'John and Isobel – Céad mile fáilte'* was scribbled on the back, 'a hundred thousand welcomes'.

Maggie peered once more at the photograph, holding it up close to the bus window to see better the weathered-looking building with its storm windows set deep in the wall, the cement path with vegetable patch on one side, drying green on the other, and the moorland stretching beyond the fence. Not a tree in sight and hardly a bush even, nothing to relieve the emptiness of the landscape. While pacing the ship's deck she'd gone up that front path a score of times at least, trying to decide how she'd introduce herself – and she'd still no idea.

Mr and Mrs Callander, John and his wife Isobel, had done their best to take up a happy-family pose on the front step of their new property – arms round each other, the promise of kindness showing in their faces, and Callander squinting into the sun's glare with a hand raised to shield his eyes. Maggie tilted the photo to catch the best light.

'CLACHTARVIE!' The driver had to call out several times before she realised she'd come to her stop – she'd been far too engrossed in what she could make out of Mr Callander's face and in the cheerful smile his wife was giving to the camera.

The bus drove off leaving her in the middle of nowhere. There was a scattering of cottages, the peat bog, and a clear-sounding *peewit, peewit* from high up in the sky – no bird to be seen, however. Ahead lay the dazzling sheen of sunlight caught by the sea. Like the landscape in the black-and-white photograph but friendlier-looking, and with the pleasing warmth of the sun on her skin.

To her left an unpaved road led down towards a bay. There were no street signs, but this had to be the right direction. She began walking. The houses on either side stood a good fifty feet apart, each on its own patch of ground. She made her way down the street inspecting them as she passed. It was hot now, but with a chill undercurrent blowing in from the sea. At the last house on the right, she stopped. Yes, here was the place she knew so well from the photograph. Someone had made a start on pebble-dashing the front wall and small stones lay heaped nearby. Maybe she could offer to help them finish? A life-sized jigsaw where all the pieces were the same – easy! The wreck of a dark-blue car, wheel-less, with its axles up on blocks and one of the side doors missing, squatted over by the fence. Its bumper trailed in the uncut grass.

Pushing the gate so that it swung open to admit her . . . Waiting for it to close with a dull *thwack* of wood against wood . . .

Forcing herself the three, four, five, six steps up the path.

The door turned out to be varnished a dark brown. There was no bell. She put down her suitcase.

A deep breath. Her hand lifted ready to knock . . .

Her last chance to turn back.

Her firm rap on the wood panel echoed inside the house. Such a dull hollowness was nothing like the cheerful tongue-and-clapper jingle made by a city tenement doorbell swinging on its wire to announce that she'd arrived at a friend's and was waiting downstairs, eager to be let in. Back home, in a decade that had seen parts of Edinburgh and Glasgow turned to rubble, the purely physical summons of bare knuckles battering on someone's door would have suggested urgency and alarm, a warning that something terrible was happening or had already taken place – a house bombed, the danger of fire, escaped gas or the building's imminent collapse. Here on the Outer Hebrides, however, her knock would hold no such threat. It was a friendly tap on a door, nothing more. This was how things were done here and always had been, she told herself, a commonplace gesture of neighbourliness. Having knocked once, she lifted her hand away . . . and took a step back.

No need to repeat the knock. Maggie could hear someone coming, calling ahead in a rush of Gaelic as they made their way from the back of the house. In time, she thought to herself, she'd probably have to learn the language.

The door swung open. A man stood in the half-darkness of the interior. John Callander, it had to be. Red hair, red face. Smaller than in the photograph, dressed in a collarless shirt and waistcoat. Slippers. What had probably been intended as words of welcome were broken off in mid-phrase.

Now they were face to face, was he about to greet her, to smile and shake her hand?

To step aside, perhaps, ready to throw the door wide open?

Was he about to take charge of her suitcase, and invite her in?

Was he hell.

John Callander stared at her and said nothing. There was a movement in the dimly lit hallway behind him, a suggestion of sweeping yellow hair and pale-coloured jersey. This would be Mrs Callander. Leaning against the inside of the door, she, too, seemed in no hurry to do anything.

Maggie looked from one to the other and back again. Red man. Yellow woman. John and wife Isobel. Their combined silence blocking her entry.

She cleared her throat. 'Hello, I'm Maggie Davies. I've come from Edinburgh and—'

'Yes, we know who *you* are . . .'

The contempt in his voice, the disgust.

As if a charge of electricity had found a hateful circuitry already in place inside her, she felt her body seize, her every muscle lock tight. She couldn't breathe even, the next few seconds swelling up in her chest, her throat – a solid, choking mass.

'. . . and we know *all* about you.' Callander took a step back into his house. And slammed the door in her face.

Stumbling over to the derelict car to slump against its rusted bonnet, tears running down her face. Not even the strength to wipe them away.

The partly pebble-dashed stonework, the vegetables planted in their rows, the trackless moorland, the very sky itself – everything around her suddenly reduced to a meaningless slapdash.

She'd come to where the world stops.

She stayed there.

It was not until later, when she heard the sound of a vehicle going past on the main road, that she glanced up to see a van crossing the featureless landscape – she watched it getting smaller and smaller, its windscreen catching the sun's glare for a moment as the road curved. Finally it vanished. At one point a teenage boy wearing an oversized army coat came out of the cottage opposite. He took his bicycle from where it leant against the wall and wheeled it across the garden before mounting. A last wave to someone at the window before he set off across the peat bog, his too-long coat tails flapping with each pedal thrust. Like the car earlier, he too grew smaller and smaller as he headed further into the flat, empty landscape. Finally he too vanished.

The Callanders remained indoors all this time. What did they do while waiting for her to leave? Did they flick through the newspaper? Listen to the radio? Read their Bibles? Did they glance at each other every few minutes: *Has she gone yet?* Or did they sit completely at their ease, secure in their faith, confident that sooner or later they'd hear her footsteps retreat back down the path, followed by the *thwack* of their wooden gate as she took herself and the disgrace of her unwanted pregnancy out of their lives – helter-skeltering herself straight back to Hell where she belonged?

When Maggie eventually managed to haul herself to her feet and stumble out onto the unpaved road, she was aware of being observed from behind the tight little window – no doubt the Callanders were making sure she hadn't left her suitcase behind.

With only the unseen *peewit* for company, she dragged herself and her suitcase all the way up to the main road. Four hours later, a bus appeared. She stared out the window all the way back to Stornoway, seeing nothing.

Having returned to the bench where she'd eaten her fish supper the night before, Maggie sat watching the comings and goings on the small ferry tied up at the dockside. From time to time smoke came in casual puffs from its funnel. Through the large window she could see two men on the bridge having a long conversation. Passengers weren't boarding yet. Every few minutes a red-headed sailor staggered up the gangway carrying a box or a crate; the bulkier-looking packages he balanced on his shoulders. Another sailor was coiling rope on the rear deck while a third looked on, smoking a cigarette. Everyone, it seemed, had something to do.

Should she take the ferry back to the mainland, then the train to Edinburgh? She was in good time to board, if she wanted to.

But did she?

Back home? Back to her parents?

Back to Edinburgh, at least?

Stay on Lewis?

For what?

But . . . back to Edinburgh?

After a while she felt like she'd been sitting there for ever, her suitcase at her feet.

Eventually the small ship cast off, and soon there was only a slow trail of smoke drifting above the bay. The faraway rumble of the engines grew fainter and fainter.

Why hadn't she gone on board? She didn't know.

Why had she stayed? She didn't know that either.

She got to her feet and made her way along to Mrs Stewart's boarding house.

Early next morning Maggie was woken by the sound of heavy rain. She climbed out of bed and closed her window. Standing barefoot on the cold linoleum, she watched the fishing boats manoeuvre towards the harbour mouth before passing, one by one, out into the open sea. The grey-white puff-puff-puffs from their smokestacks were flattened by the wind before being taken up, tossed into the air and shredded to nothing. The steady *thud-thud-thud* of the engines was blown towards the shore, and whenever an extra-strong gust rattled the glass in its frame she pressed her hand against the pane, and stilled it.

Soon enough the storm seemed to become a live thing trying to force its way into the house. She could hear it battering its fists on the downstairs door and hurling itself at the walls, but she knew she was safe. Mrs Stewart's house was pre-war, and by a good couple of centuries. It had outlasted many storms and would see this one out, too, no problem.

The floor shook so much she almost expected to be lifted off her feet or else to see the walls billow in and out like the sails of a long-ago ship far out at sea . . .

Yes, *far out at sea* – that was where she really was. No land in sight and her only cargo her unborn child. Men, it seemed, always had some sort of harbour to make for. That was the nature of *their* world – a map of place names like Normandy, Amiens, Berlin. For men it was enough to identify aims and objectives, and then draw co-ordinates – that done, and with bayonets fixed, they marched, marched, marched into the future, whatever the cost. But for her, after that reception at the Callanders', what destination remained?

Even though it was mainly the Leith docks that had been bombed, everyone's life and routine had been smashed beyond repair. Something had got into the works – the grit of countless deaths, perhaps – and a new kind of routine had taken over. She herself had worked long hours in a factory making bombs she knew would kill and maim, she'd packed ammunition that would cause death to someone's husband or son.

The last fishing boat having gone, she returned to bed. It was only five o'clock. Back under the blankets she lay listening to the storm. Even before getting herself pregnant, what had she been hoping for? During the last year of the war when their housemaid Annie had left to join the WRACs, Maggie had been expected to assist her mother in running the house. She'd cooked and cleaned, she'd scrubbed floors and brushed shoes, beaten carpets, polished brass work and mopped the outside steps. She was given pocket money for tram fare, for the pictures and for the odd evening out at the dancing. By the time peace was declared, she had turned twenty-five. Would this be the way of it from now on? she'd sometimes wondered as she passed through the hall on her way back to the kitchen, carrying the dirty dishes, her footsteps falling all too readily in step with the slow relentless *tick . . . tick . . . tick . . .* of the grandfather clock standing at the bottom of the stairs.

Even when she joined her friends in the packed dance halls on Princes Street or at Fairley's Ballroom at the top of Leith Walk, she'd often been aware of that merciless *tick . . . tick . . . tick . . .* inside her, as if she herself had become the empty sounding-board for the hours and days and years being relentlessly sliced off her life. Twenty-five became twenty-six, became twenty-seven. Whatever the music, whatever the band, more and more she found herself alone at the edge of the floor, stranded there, waiting to be asked to dance and waiting in vain. Every man, of course, was guaranteed a partner. Ten times over. She was marking time merely.

She turned twenty-eight, twenty-nine, thirty . . .

He wore a tie-pin that was probably some kind of army crest. Having persuaded her to remain on the floor for a second dance, a slow waltz, he told her he was called Danny and invited her to have a drink with him at the bar. As they stood in the crush, he said how he'd sometimes pictured a girl like her when things had got *difficult*. Taking her hand, he murmured that he'd been lucky to get through it all and had come home hoping to find someone special – did she know what he meant? While he rubbed the back of her hand, almost nervously, unconsciously perhaps even, he'd added in a shy voice that he'd imagined someone who, in their turn, had been waiting and keeping themselves for someone like him. He didn't want one of these would-be glamorous girls who paraded about like they had film-star looks and were interested only in silk stockings, cigarettes and ration coupons. He leant nearer and whispered that he wanted a quiet girl, someone trusting, affectionate – someone to care for and who would care for him in return. This was what he told her as they stood sipping their drinks between dances that first evening.

And, yes, *she*'d been exactly the kind of girl he'd wanted – a girl so desperate to get away from her parents' home that she'd make herself believe every single word he told her. That she'd trust him, totally.

She pushed aside the covers and placed both hands on her stomach. Just over three months' pregnant but nothing showed yet, not even the slightest bump. The Callanders must have been warned. Having thrown her out of the house, her parents must have noticed the photograph was missing and written to them, letting them know of their daughter's shameful 'condition' and expressing their own church-going views on the matter. Girls became women became wives became mothers – that was the proper way of it, the only way. If a girl couldn't wait, then she had to marry whoever made her pregnant. Call it divine intervention, call it Russian roulette.

Maggie punched her pillow, then lay staring up at the ceiling. She'd been so ashamed. She'd thought only about leaving Edinburgh, running away as fast and as far as she could – it was as simple as that. Running away to where no one really knew her or knew anything about her.

What had she been hoping for, coming here – the hundred thousand welcomes?

At seven she dressed and went down to breakfast.

Out of the dining room window she could see the storm was

easing, but the sky remained weighted with dark clouds and a watery daylight that threatened more rain. Once again she seemed to be the only guest. The stiff-backed dining chair sighed as she sat down and the others stared blankly back at her, without passing remark. The dark mahogany dresser had clearly run out of conversation years ago.

This grim silent room. Outside, weathered to a complete indifference to her or anything about her, were the rain-lashed streets and buildings of Stornoway. In Edinburgh she'd have been getting ready to catch the tram to join the Saturday morning bustle of Princes Street, in and out of Jenners, PT's, J&R Allen's, Binn's. A pot of tea in Mackie's or Crawford's. Some chatter and gossip while soaking up the sun on the grassy slopes of the Gardens.

No. No. No.

Maggie took a deep breath and tapped her knuckles on the polished table as though to call a meeting to order. She had propositions to consider, decisions to make.

Top of the agenda – Item One: Should she remain on Lewis, or leave?

Straightforward enough, surely.

As she ate her breakfast, she asked each of the empty chairs in turn for their advice and was about to consult the dresser when Mrs Stewart entered.

'Another storm on its way, Mrs Davies. Some of the fishing boats are coming back so you can be sure it'll be a big one – these men need every penny they can haul out of the sea. We're in for it, right enough.'

'And the ferry?'

'Cancelled most likely. And tomorrow is the Sabbath.'

So that was that.

By noon the rain was coming down heavier than ever. There was a knock on her bedroom door. It was Mrs Stewart.

'You're not telling me you're going out in that, Mrs Davies?' she said. 'If you don't mind eating in the kitchen, you're welcome to have a bite of lunch with us.'

'That's very kind of you, but—' Maggie started to protest.

'I'll not take no for an answer.' Mrs Stewart smiled. 'See you downstairs in half an hour.'

Over a bowl of broth with bread and cheese for afters, Mrs Stewart asked all the questions and Maggie did her best to make up the answers. No mention of her being pregnant, of course. She'd lost her husband a year ago almost to the day, she told them. A car accident. Her parents were no longer alive, killed when the family house was bombed during the war. Her brothers had been killed too. She announced this as an afterthought, to help keep things simple. She'd been the only survivor.

Once she got into her stride, her story seemed to tell itself; it flowed out easily and cheerfully almost. She'd come to Lewis for a short break to help get herself through the first anniversary of her loss. Her poor husband – she christened him Alfred for some reason and had difficulty keeping a straight face every time she mentioned his name – had been very brave. She described how *Alfred* had suffered, how *Alfred* had never complained, how *Alfred* had lingered for several months, needing her constant care. Before she could stop herself, she heard herself adding that *Alfred* had had a beard that just grew longer and longer as he lay there. She had to trim it so he'd not get himself tangled in the blankets when he turned over in bed. Seeing Mrs Stewart's rather puzzled look, she quickly went on to tell how *Alfred* had died in her arms. She spoke brokenly, following her words with a few moments' respectful silence.

Mrs Stewart was very sympathetic, even more so when she learned there had been no children.

Maggie's offer to help clear the table was declined; instead she was urged to stay, enjoy another cup of tea and chat with son Michael.

Later, when she was getting up to leave, Michael asked if he might 'read' her face again 'so's to help me remember, Mrs Davies.'

She let him, naturally.

The rain having turned into a steady drizzle, she borrowed an umbrella and went for a long walk. There was no ferry boat tied up at the quayside. Instead, a handwritten notice announced all sailings were cancelled till Monday. She felt strangely relieved. No need for a decision, not today anyway.

On her return to the boarding house she was told that, unless she had other plans, there would be a place laid for her at the kitchen table that evening. 'Nothing fancy, you understand, Mrs Davies. Simple fare.'

The meal of herring and potatoes, with tinned rice pudding for dessert, was rounded off with more questions.

No, she didn't own the flat where she now lived. When she returned to Edinburgh she'd have to start looking for somewhere smaller.

She would have to find a job, too.

Had she ever worked?

Only making bombs.

When Michael asked what colour her hair was and what she was wearing, Mrs Stewart interrupted the awkwardness of her reply to say that their guest was being far too modest.

'She's a bonny lass. Nice face, nice figure and just coming into her mid-twenties (she winked at Maggie, who'd been about to protest, and put a finger to her lips). They'll not be letting her leave the island, you can be sure of that.'

'Mrs Stewart, I—'

'Never heed me, lass, just teasing . . . But maybe you'll be finding yourself staying on the island just that wee bit longer than you planned!'

'Mother! Don't embarrass our guest. I must apologise, Mrs Davies, my mother can sometimes be rather—'

'There's no problem, really. I can take a joke.' She glanced back across at Michael but, of course, he hadn't noticed her quick smile, and never would.

Later, when Maggie said she would go upstairs, Michael asked if he might be allowed to pass his hands over her face one more time. 'It'll help me really picture you.'

'So, you're coming to join us at the kirk, Mrs Davies?' Mrs Stewart greeted her at the foot of the stairs, while her son stood waiting at the front door. Both of them were dressed as for a funeral – their best black relieved only by the red edging on the older woman's bible and by the white of Michael's stick.

'Church? Oh, I hadn't thought.' Then Maggie had an inspiration: 'The service will be in Gaelic, won't it?'

'Aye, it will, but—'

'Mrs Davies has no need to sit through two hours of boredom. It's a glorious summer's day that God has given her. She should go out and enjoy it.'

Which she did.

Next morning, after breakfast, Mrs Stewart called up to say that she'd be off to the shops shortly and wouldn't be back till after twelve. 'Kitchen table's set for three.'

Before she could reply, Maggie heard the front door being shut.

She planned to take a walk into town to find out when the normal ferry sailings would be resumed and was getting herself ready to leave when she heard someone come out of the sitting room. Next, they were coming up the stairs.

Quickly, she crossed to the mirror that was set in the wardrobe door.

A light tap on the door. The slight hesitancy in his voice: 'Mrs Davies? . . . Maggie?'

Giving her hair a pat, smoothing down the front of her blouse.

'Maggie? I was wondering if you'd like to come down and join me for a cup of tea?'

Trying to re-fasten the clasp of an awkward brooch in the mirror, wrong-handedly.

'That'd be nice, Michael. Be with you in a few minutes.'

Stopping herself, hand poised in mid-air. *What was she doing? Michael wouldn't notice if she wasn't looking her –*

Maggie came into the kitchen to find Michael pouring out a cup of tea for her. The wooden table had been laid with teacups and saucers, side plates, milk jug, sugar bowl. He placed the teapot on the tea-stand and covered it with an embroidered tea-cosy.

'I forgot the biscuits. Would you like one?'

'That's kind of you. But, Michael, please don't trouble yourself to—'

'It's no trouble. Have a seat. Help yourself to milk and sugar.'

Maggie watched in fascination as Michael crossed to a cupboard, opened the door and, without any hesitation, selected and brought out a large tin. He returned to the table, took his seat, removed the lid. So surely did he move about the kitchen performing his various tasks that she would never have known he was blind.

'There should be a couple of snowballs left in there as well as some digestives. One of them'll have your name on it.'

'But how can you – ?' she began before she could stop herself.

'Oh, I keep an eye on the snowballs!' he joked. 'But really, Maggie, just because I'm blind doesn't mean I'm completely helpless. I *know* this house, because I've learnt it. So long as things remain in the same place I'm fine. Quite independent really. In fact, when Mother had to keep to her bed for a few days last winter with a bad cold I managed to look after her perfectly well, and with no outside help. Cooking, washing, cleaning – the lot! You might say that my blindness didn't make a blind bit of difference! Slightly slower than the average home help perhaps, but no less thorough, so I'm told – at least for a man!' He laughed. 'I know the streets of Stornoway, too, and the shops. If you fancy, we can go for a walk through the town afterwards to let you get properly acquainted with the place.'

Half an hour later they had left the house and were walking along the quayside. It was turning into a beautiful summer's day and, for the first time in months, Maggie felt herself relax as they strolled along together, Michael's white stick *tap-tap-tapping* out a path for them.

He took her to the Town Hall, to the bank where he'd worked before the war; he showed her his favourite bar. Then, having come round almost full-circle, they returned to the harbour.

'Along here is a bench where I sometimes go to sit in the mornings, to feel the sun on my face.'

The instant Michael had spoken, Maggie was certain he was about to lead her to the very same bench where she'd eaten fish and chips that first evening she'd arrived.

Which he did.

Once they'd sat down, Michael touched her lightly on the arm: 'Tell me what you see, Maggie – and give me colours, lots and lots of colours.'

'Well, it really is a lovely day, hardly a cloud in the sky – in the blue, blue sky, I should say. The sea is flat, totally calm. The water looks greenish and shiny with the sun on it. There are two fishing boats at the quayside, one's natural wood with a yellow cabin, the other has a black-painted cabin. Just along from us, a fisherman in a dark brown jersey and with green wellingtons up to his knees is sitting next to a heap of lobster pots; he's doing something with a net, untangling it or mending it. There are white seagulls, a red van . . .'

She felt a sudden need to close her eyes. Like she was trying to imagine what Michael saw, sitting here beside her on the bench on this beautiful sunny day. Darkness. Pitch-black darkness, a night that for him went on and on and on, and that he awoke to every morning.

She just wanted to feel what it was like for him.

Didn't she?

No.

That wasn't it. Not really.

Rather, it felt like –

Like she'd stepped into one of those screened confessionals for Catholics, where they speak to an unseen priest.

She'd closed her eyes because she wanted to confess, was that it? To tell him she was pregnant? Tell him, and be forgiven?

She wanted to tell him – yes. She *needed* to. All morning she'd felt that need get stronger and stronger, until it had become almost unbearable. Like a threat, it had now taken over everything she could see and hear – the harbour, the sky, their sitting together on the bench. It had built up inside her until her whole world seemed to shudder from moment to moment with the force of what remained unspoken.

But there was no reason to tell him. What would it matter to *him* that she was pregnant?

She had to, though. She couldn't help it.

Her eyes tight shut, she was about to speak when –

'I was driving a British Army truck in a convoy across France. It was a summer's day, Maggie, just like this. Blue skies and hardly a cloud to be seen, exactly how you described

33

it. Overhead the German fighters were strafing us, sometimes Stukas dive-bombed. My lorry got hit. Seems I was thrown clear; they found me crawling on my hands and knees along the ditch beside the road. Not that I remember anything, except waking up . . .'

Maggie had to stop herself from reaching over to touch the back of his hand.

'I'm so sorry, Michael. It must have been so . . . so terrible. I can't begin to imagine how you . . .'

'It was seven years ago. I've had seven years more than the other men who were in the lorry, and I get the gift of an extra day every morning. Like today – and here I am sitting on this bench in the sun with you, and enjoying the blue sky, the red van, the fisherman's dark brown jersey and his green waders. All thanks to you!'

Without thinking about it, she gave his arm a comforting squeeze.

When they returned, Michael asked if he could read her face again. 'To keep in touch,' he smiled.

Afterwards he didn't step away.

'Would you like to try? See what it feels like?'

She closed her eyes.

There was no tremble in his hand as he guided her fingers across his smoothly shaved cheek. But, as she stood there, *I'm pregnant, I'm pregnant* kept hammering over and over in her head. All she could feel was the effort it was taking her to stop from screaming the words out loud.

In bed that night she allowed herself to relive the touch of

Michael's fingertips, their warmth as they'd traced out the smoothness of her forehead, her eyelids, cheeks, lips, the curve down to her neck.

Suppose he had begun to stroke her hair, suppose he had taken her in his arms and kissed her? *Pregnant. Pregnant. Pregnant.*

The spell of good weather continued. A few days later, while they were enjoying a picnic of sandwiches and a thermos flask of tea on their bench, Maggie heard herself say: 'I don't know what's happening between us, Michael . . .'

She knew perfectly well, of course – what was happening to *her*, certainly. She was falling in love. She couldn't help herself.

'. . . but it's good. It feels very good.'

Next thing, he had fumbled for her hand and taken it. Raised it to his lips.

That night she lay awake for hours remembering what happened next. When they'd kissed, she'd longed – longed with a desperation she'd never known before – for his kiss to be all there was to her life.

She stood at the top of the stairs one morning, gazing around at the seascape print on the wall, the runner carpet, varnished floorboards, the view of the harbour through the small storm window, the arrangement of flowers in a vase . . . Was it possible that her days would begin with a glance like this out of the low window to check on the weather, with her noticing some mornings that the flowers looked a bit tired and could do with being replaced?

§

Mrs Stewart insisted on always setting a place for her at table. 'Don't embarrass me,' she'd say whenever Maggie brought up the subject of payment for her lodgings.

One afternoon she heard him whisper: 'I'm so happy we've found each other, Maggie.'

Yes, she answered into herself. *Yes*. Then she said it aloud: 'Yes, Michael. So am I.'

I'm pregnant. I'm pregnant.

Next moment, she'd blurted the words out. Told him how it had happened. Then closed her eyes, waiting for his reply. When it came, it was short.

'We'll manage.'

The following afternoon they almost bumped into the Callanders. She and Michael were walking along the main street having been to the butcher's and greengrocer's – mince, potatoes, onions and carrots for the evening meal – and were making for the baker's, the last on their list.

The Callanders were approaching from the opposite direction – Mr Callander with a black and green tartan shopping bag in his right hand. Noticing her, they came to a halt right outside the shop. They stared. Not a word was spoken.

'The baker's, Maggie, and then we're done,' said Michael.

'It looks pretty busy in there, Michael.' She glanced across at the Callanders standing side by side only a few yards away. 'Let's go to our bench at the harbour instead. We'll get the bread later on.' She pulled at his arm to steer him back the way they'd come.

'Carrying these bags? No chance.' Michael laughed. 'A few minutes' queuing won't matter. We can get ourselves a couple of doughnuts to have on the bench – my treat!' He tapped his way past the Callanders and went into the baker's. Maggie followed.

When they came out a few minutes later, the Callanders were nowhere to be seen.

Michael turned to her: 'Thought you said it was busy?'

'I just wanted to go and sit in the sun with you.' She squeezed his arm. 'And now we've doughnuts to share as well!'

That evening she came downstairs to find Michael already seated at the kitchen table. There was no sign of Mrs Stewart. To her surprise, one of the place settings had been removed. Was the older woman, in her most encouraging way, leaving the two of them to enjoy an intimate dinner by themselves?

Before sitting down, she went round to him. As always, his gaze was fixed unwaveringly on nothing.

'Hello, Michael.' She raised her hand and was about to read his face in greeting before kissing him, when she became aware of his hand fumbling to take hers.

'Maggie?'

He grasped her fingers and began stroking them. 'Mother met a Clachtarvie woman today in the street.'

'Your mother met – who?'

He remained staring straight at her, sightlessly. 'Oh Maggie. I'm so – so sorry.'

Then she understood. The Callanders.

For several seconds they remained hand in hand, without speaking. 'Everybody knows everybody here, Maggie. And knows everything about everybody. We'll need to—'

'We don't provide dinner for guests, *Miss* Davies.' Mrs Stewart was standing in the doorway. 'There's nothing for you here.'

'Mother? Maggie and I are—'

'This is my house, as well you know, and I'm the one who runs it – as well you know, too.' The older woman advanced into the kitchen. 'You're not welcome, *Miss* Davies – and I doubt you'll be welcome anywhere on the island, not any more. Coming here, abusing our trust.'

'Mrs Stewart, I never meant to—'

'Bringing your sinfulness into our house, bringing your *shame*.'

'How dare you, I—'

'But I know my Christian duty. The next ferry is tomorrow morning. Keep to your room till then. We'll be well rid of you, and cheap at the price.' Mrs Stewart turned away to see to a pot on the stove. 'Michael? If you're ready for your soup . . .'

Michael got to his feet and came round from behind the table to stand beside Maggie, his hand on her shoulder. 'No, mother. Maggie and I are—'

'Not a word, Michael. Nothing's changed. Nothing that I can see. Our life might not be easy but we manage, you and I. We don't need the likes of—' She switched to Gaelic. Not singsong Gaelic.

'But, Mrs Stewart. Michael and I—'

The Gaelic continued.

'Please, Mrs Stewart—'

'Your room, *Miss* Davies.' The older woman had taken a step towards her, soup ladle in one hand. 'You'll be getting your bill and I expect it paid in full before you leave.' Then the Gaelic was resumed.

'But Mrs—'

'Your room, I said.'

'Don't you dare speak to me like—'

'This is my house and I will speak in any way I choose.'

Then Gaelic, Gaelic, Gaelic.

Ten minutes later, leaving mother and son to rage at each other, Maggie went upstairs. She stood at the window, staring out at the harbour where the early evening sun hung above the slow-lapping water. The argument down in the kitchen continued for over an hour. Lying on her bed, staring up at the ceiling, she listened to it all, to every last incomprehensible word.

Then came silence. Then the rattle of pans, the rush of tap water.

At one point during the evening an envelope was pushed under her door. Her bill.

It was shortly after midnight when Maggie became aware of someone outside her room. She heard the handle being turned and the door softly opening. Then being closed.

Footsteps were approaching the side of her bed –

'Maggie?'

Michael was leaning over her. She could feel his breath warm on her cheek.

'Maggie?'

Without speaking, she reached up to stroke his face in

greeting. They kissed . . . and in the darkness Michael's blinded country became hers.

Maggie got up early. Very, very early. She dried her eyes, washed her face and dressed as quickly as she could. After she'd finished packing, she put on her coat. Then, suitcase in one hand and shoes in the other, she left her room.

Having tiptoed along the corridor to the top of the stairs, she paused for a moment. Listened.

Quite certain at last that the rest of the house was still asleep, she went downstairs.

On the hall table she left two single pound notes under her key, two pounds that she couldn't really afford. Then checked herself in the mirror, dabbed her eyes again. Took a deep breath.

Once outside on the doorstep she wanted to slam the front door behind her, slam it full-force – but managed to stop herself. Then, having pulled it shut, she wanted to thump her fists against its hardwood panels, and to kick and kick and kick.

Again she stopped herself.

She had to leave. She *knew* she had to leave. End of story.

In tears again, she made her way along the silent street to the ferry terminal. An hour later she was on board and heading back to the mainland.

SUNDAY

HIGH-BACKED ARMCHAIRS LINED up against the day-room walls. Meals, meds, bath, bed. The bay window keeping everything else out – the front lawn, the bush, the small tree, the big tree, the red yellow blue flowers, the visitors' car park, the visitors' cars. The main street, the people, the traffic, shop-windows, tenement windows. The sky that's no longer yours. The TV that's always on.

The first time the man you think of as Tom's friend brought you here for a look round the place, you heard someone say it felt like a waiting room. Waiting for what? you joked. A joke you always remember when you come through after breakfast to find every single minute and every long hour of the day ahead already gathered here, waiting for you. The *dayroom* – the very name makes you shiver every time you take your seat.

Thursday? Monday? Saturday? Different names for the one same day that slides backwards and forwards along the one same week that never comes to an end, but keeps starting over keeps starting over keeps starting over . . .

You'll be safe now, Maggie. By day you have your own seat two places down from the Murray sisters, and at night you have your own bed. Here the corridors are all one day long. The same day.

Were the Murrays twins from the start? Seated side by side, feet splayed out flat on the floor, hands crossed on their laps, coat-hanger shoulders, silver-thread hair. Staring, staring into space – rabbits caught in a set of headlights that no one else can see. Dorothy seated in the corner calling out *Wait for me, Mother. Wait for me.* MOTHER? MOTHER? *Wait for me* . . . all day long. The Murrays, Dorothy. No one speaks by name to any of the other women lined up in their chairs, and the women never speak back. Not sleeping, not waking – but dreaming. Yes, you hope they're dreaming.

And the man of your dreams? You know that when he appears in the doorway, he's going to ask one of you to dance. In the end, that's why you're all here.

Fred Astaire top hat, bow-tie and tails like he's stepped out of a black-and-white film, he'll pause for a moment as if taking a good look round – searching, probably, for the next Ginger Rogers. Scouting out the talent, it used to be called at Fairley's Ballroom and the other dance halls on Leith Walk and along Princes Street. Sweeping his hat from his head, he gives the entire room a *boulevardier* bow of such well-practised elegance that you can imagine the intake of breath on all sides. As he drifts round the edge of the floor, his black patent leather shoes drip with the sunlight that's pooled here and there on the polished lino. Like he's wading through the lushness of strings coming from an unseen orchestra. Lingering before each one of you in turn, a tilt of the head, a knowing smile here, a few softly spoken words there – who will he choose to be his partner for this special once-in-a-lifetime dance?

One day, of course, he'll stop when he reaches you. And

it'll be Michael. Yes, you *know* it will be him. You'll know by the touch of his fingertips upon your face, their gentleness, his sightless eyes brimming with—

'Med time, Mrs Stewart.'

While murmuring your name he'll draw you up into his arms. Shut your eyes, Maggie, and then you'll feel him close, so very close. Keep them shut – his hand's resting lightly on your waist as he birls you across the room and back, up and down the floor until all the rag-tag, long-ago years whirl round and round the pair of you in a swirling blur of—

'Mrs Stewart.'

Faster and faster you go, your feet no longer touching the ground—

'Med time, Mrs Stewart.'

Like you're dancing on air, on sunlight itself—

'MED TIME. MRS STEWART.'

No music, no Michael, no being swept round in his—

'Not for me. I'm Davies. Maggie Davies. How many times do I have to tell you?'

'Maggie, then. Meds. Drink now, Maggie. One . . . two . . . Drink. Today Sunday. Today Mr Magic come.'

'Who?'

'Mr Magic he called – yes? He come for you today. You, Maggie, you stay sit and he come. Like he say he come. No worries.'

'Mr Magic?'

'All the Sundays. When you first here he say he come all the Sundays and today Sunday.'

'It's a mix-up calling me Mrs Stewart, you know. Real mixter-maxter. Names really matter, Donna. Can't be too careful with meds. If you give me Mrs Stewart's meds, then what about her? What's poor Mrs Stewart getting?'

Whenever you ask them to point Mrs Stewart out to you, they roll their eyes and shake their heads.

The only man here is called Slow Peter. They've told you another name, but you know that name's not right. So you keep to Slow Peter. You *know* Slow Peter. They've told you he'll fix leaks and come when your bedroom window's jammed or a light bulb's gone. You know his real name even if no one else does. You know all their names – Slow Peter, Donna, Mrs Saunders, Beryl . . . When you tell them, trying to help keep them right, they just smile and say *Suit yourself, Maggie.* So you do.

'Hello, Mum.'

Someone's bent down to kiss your forehead, leaning too close for you to see their face. Calling you his mother, like he's lost his own.

You'd like to call him 'Michael', to say the name to someone, to hear it spoken out loud.

He's taken your hand like he wants to keep good hold while he talks.

So let him.

Talk and talk and talk. And sometimes you talk back at him. About the Murrays and Dorothy, about Slow Peter and Mrs Saunders, about Donna and Beryl, about the things on TV—

'Yes, Mum, when I'm on TV I'm called Mr Magic, remember. Been going a lot longer than *The X Factor*! You've seen me sometimes—'

You manage to keep looking over his shoulder. 'That letter's made her cry. Look!' Pointing to what's happening on the screen: 'Look at that poor woman – imagine someone writing to her so as to make her cry. Like they were really *wanting* to make her cry.'

'Mum—' He's started to stroke your arm. 'Mum, please. It's only something on TV, like when you see me make things disappear, playing cards and flowers and even people sometimes. Remember me telling you how I created that illusion about the—'

'Heartless it is. A disgrace. A real disgrace.'

'Don't get upset. It's nothing. Would you like me to—?'

'The poor woman. But Jean's got a cake all ready and waiting, never fear. A slice of that would cheer her up and take her mind off things. They'll be bringing it soon. Cream and jam, layers and layers of cream and jam. Real cream too, mind – all the ration coupons she could get hold of. Had to be good if we were to—' You peer over his shoulder again, half-afraid at what you might see. 'Will you look at that poor woman! Look. Look at her. LOOK AT HER!'

Tears have started running down your cheeks. Tears you make no move to wipe away.

Instead—

Struggling to get to your feet, pointing your finger at the screen: 'That poor, poor woman. CAN'T SOMEBODY DO SOMETHING? CAN'T SOMEBODY HELP HER? HELP HER HELP HER HELP HER HELP HER!'

Next moment it's all turned to horse-racing and a red-faced man talking into a microphone. Which is nothing much, so you sit down again.

§

They're closing your curtains. But it's not the woman you call Donna, who's grown up into a well-meaning lassie and always has time to stop for a word or two. It's Boss Beryl – you'd know her vicious tug-and-swish anywhere.

'Leave them, please. It's too soon. He's away making us a pot of tea. Nice man – for a man. Brought me some biscuits, too, my favourites—'

'And flowers, Maggie. Brought you flowers, too. Must have put them in a vase for you, too. See?'

'Flowers?'

Then like out of nowhere, it seems, there's suddenly a vase of flowers on the chest of drawers. You can feel the glow spreading across your face, beaming into a smile. A real grin. 'Michael? Michael's really come?'

'That his name, was it? He's long gone.'

'Don't be silly, Beryl. There's the flowers. How else would they have got here? Making us some tea. Back in a jiffy, he said.'

'Went home ages ago, Maggie.'

'HobNobs, my favourites. But you can have one, if you like.'

'An hour and more's drive back up to Edinburgh. He had to go. It's late now, Maggie. I've brought you your hot drink.'

'He was right here only a moment ago, Beryl. Right here. We were talking about . . . something. He's always talking. He's along the corridor making us both a cup of tea . . .'

'That was this afternoon, Maggie. It's nearly night now.'

'Afternoon? Night? How can it—?'

'You've had your first Sunday here and he says he'll come every Sunday afternoon just to see that you're—'

'I'm not stupid, Beryl. I'm not one of the Murrays. I'm not Dorothy. Sunday afternoon. I *know* Sunday afternoon. I understand *afternoon*. I understand *Sunday*.'

'Goodnight now, Maggie. It's your sleep time. Here's your—'

'I know Sunday. I want Sunday! Sunday! SUNDAY!'

'You need to rest and—

'SUNDAY! SUNDAY! SUNDAY!'

2

DIRTY YELLOWISH SMOKE hung over the tracks and platforms of Waverley Station, and once again Maggie found herself walking through cloud – a cloud of steam this time, of soot and perpetual twilight. Her eyes smarted and she could taste the coal dust coating her tongue. Someone jostled her, making her stumble against the bottom step of the driver's cab. Close to, a furnace-heat roar came from the engine. She breathed in the smell of hot metal and burnt oil. Steam hissed out from between the massive wheels.

'And the same to you!' she hissed back at them.

Gripping her suitcase, she pushed her way towards the ticket barrier. To her right a guard's whistle blew – another train was leaving. From all sides came the clash and grind of metal on metal, the rumble of porters' wagons, the slamming of carriage doors, and passengers shouting at each other to be heard above the din. Here was no windswept, treeless desolation – but real-life noise and bustle welcoming her back to her home city.

Having handed over her ticket, she stepped into the crowd of friends and family come to greet the new arrivals. No one would be waiting for her, but she couldn't help glancing across whenever there was a sudden cry and someone rushed forward into the open arms of someone else – wife/husband, girlfriend/

boyfriend, brother/sister, friends. She'd turn away, but wasn't always quick enough to shut out the sight of other people's happiness. At the same time, she wanted to see it, to enjoy their pleasure at being together once more – and to snatch that glimpse of an embrace, a kiss . . . of a separation healed.

Michael had asked for her photograph to keep and, even though he couldn't see, he said he could always 'read' it. At that very moment he and his mother would probably be finishing their lunch. Maggie toiled up the steep slope that led out of the station, her suitcase getting heavier at every step – they'd be sitting facing each other at the kitchen table, with its two settings. A blind man? Could she really have coped with a newborn baby, and being married to a blind man, and all the while trying to settle down to a life as Mrs Stewart number two in that house – for her mother-in-law would certainly have been number one? Should she have stood her ground? Should she have stayed and—?

In time she'd surely have learned how to—

Forget it. Taking her suitcase in both hands, she marched herself up the slope as best she could – *Forget it . . . Forget it . . . Forget it* – marched herself towards the street ahead – *Forget it . . . Forget it . . . Forget it* – past the never-ending line of taxis crawling down to drop off their passengers, their wheels thumping the cobbles, sounding their horns and belching out exhaust. As she strode along, she promised herself that when she reached the top of the slope she'd be stepping into the brightness of the very sky itself. Ahead, she could see the roof of the National Gallery outlined against a cloudless blue, then the sweeping curve of the Mound with the Bank of Scotland building so grand at the top and, beyond, the

Castle itself with its upward tumble of walls and battlements shimmering in the haze. Edinburgh seemed shaped by the sky and the sky itself by the city, and, for a moment, everything seemed possible and the future hers. She was so very, very glad to be back.

The afternoon heat rose from the paving stones. A small child bumped into her, then ran off into the crowd of shoppers. She passed a comforting hand over her stomach.

Just as when her train had been approaching the city, she again heard the rhythm of its wheels rattling over the tracks: *Somewhere to stay Somewhere to stay Somewhere to stay . . .*

But first, she thought, somewhere to eat.

With luck, she might have missed the lunchtime rush. Suitcase in hand, she hurried along Princes Street, heading to Mackie's Buttery.

So, it seemed, was everyone else.

The place was mobbed. Overcrowded. Packed. Heaving. Queue right to the door.

And hot. Hot. Hot.

Quarter of an hour later, she and her tray with its corned-beef sandwich and pot of tea had found a small round table set in a crowd of other small round tables over by the window. Having put her suitcase down beside her, she stared out at the Gardens, then up at the Castle. The Black Douglas and his men, shields tied to their backs, had actually climbed up the rock face to capture it, or was that Stirling Castle? The little she'd learnt about Scottish history when she was at school – Bruce and the spider, William Wallace being betrayed and beheaded, and then Mary Queen of Scots – was from such a long time ago. As she understood it, nothing much else had happened during the next five hundred years, except down in England. She kept meaning to read a Scottish history book, if there was such a thing. She couldn't remember ever hearing of—

'These seats taken?'

She shook her head. 'No, please—'

Three people sat down and took over her table. Mr and Mrs Bicker and little Miss Bicker.

From the start Mr Bicker was on the defence:

The choice was his, no? He'd given up the fags, but the cigarette coupons were still his. Weren't they?

Mrs Bicker said she needed shoes for work. Last year's had been soled and heeled twice – the soles and heels were now all there was. First drop of rain and she might as well go barefoot.

No one's asking you to go—

Do you *want* me to go barefoot?

It's not a question of—

So you *do* want me to go barefoot? Soled and heeled twice, I'm telling you. First drop of rain and I might as well go barefoot. And as for Annie's shoes . . .

Mrs Bicker kept at it.

Meanwhile Young Annie Bicker sat and stared, watching every single mouthful as Maggie finished her sandwich.

Only a few sips of tea remained.

Having remained politely silent so far, Young Annie now spoke up: 'You got any, missus?'

'Pardon?'

'Coupons for sweeties. I like sweeties.'

'No, I'm sorry I can't help. A real shame if you're—'

But Young Annie had already turned away.

Maggie finished her tea and mumbled a goodbye as she stood up. She grabbed her suitcase that was now wedged between Mr Bicker's chair and her own. She jerked it free. No one paid any attention. She might as well have been invisible.

Leaving the Bickers to each other was surely a good start to the rest of the day.

Somewhere to stay Somewhere to stay Somewhere to stay . . .

She was crossing Princes Street intending to buy an *Evening News* from the paper seller at the top of the steps leading down to the Gardens when—

NEWHAVEN was written at the front of the tram.

Next moment she found herself sitting downstairs in her favourite seat behind the driver, her suitcase stowed under the stairs. She was certain her parents would slam the door in her face, but, then again, they might not. They'd had time to cool down, to think better about things and about her. It would be different. There was surely more to the world than a corridor running between Stornoway and Edinburgh, a corridor with a slammed-shut door at either end? Yet here she was, going down its spiteful length once more as if she couldn't help herself. But Newhaven was her home. She'd been born there. She'd gone up and down the same front steps every day for the last thirty years near enough. Ten thousand times up and down. This would make it her ten thousandth and first time – and it was going to be different.

If she changed her mind, she could get off at any stop. Any stop at all.

The tram trundled along Princes Street towards the East End, past the Waverley Market and the North British Hotel before sweeping left down into Leith Street, past Fairley's Ball-room where the squaddies and sailors still battled out the war with each other, not that she'd ever be going there again. Then past the Playhouse cinema where the organist on his platform rose up through the floor to play during the interval, past tree-lined Elm Row and into Leith Walk proper. Yes, this was her city. Here, at least, she knew she belonged.

The best way of not getting the front door slammed in her face . . . was to walk straight in.

Through the vestibule door's stippled glass she could see the familiar hall, the hat stand, the curved hall-table against the wall with the oval mirror above, the grandfather clock, the staircase going up to the bedrooms.

From the sitting room straight across came the sounds of a football match on the radio. Her father would be in his arm-chair, following every kick of the game. Her mother would be in there, too, reading the *Scotsman* or knitting.

Ever so slowly Maggie inched open the vestibule door and stepped into the main hall. She took her time easing the snib back into place, making sure there was no tell-tale *click*.

She was now inside. She was back home.

So far so good.

She put down her suitcase at the bottom of the stairs.

The measured *tick . . . tick . . . tick* of the grandfather clock, the faint sounds of the football match, the smell of the freshly polished floor – this was her home on a Saturday af-ternoon.

A last-minute check in the hall mirror. The light was poor. A quick comb through her hair and giving it a pat. Some fresh lipstick? But what if she smeared? She didn't need a wounded-looking mouth, a crazed and begging-looking mouth. What she wanted was a war-mouth, a blood-red snarl of a mouth, to show her parents she was no longer their dutiful daughter, no longer their little girl with no life of her own and no plans for her future but theirs. She'd be a mother herself by the end of the year. Like it or not, she was their equal.

She snap-shut her lipstick, pocketed it, then marched firmly across the parquet floor. Grasping the handle, she took a deep breath and threw open the sitting-room door, stepping into the comfortable predictability of her parents' Saturday afternoon.

Her mother looked up, startled. Knitting needles *click-clicking, click-clicking, click-clicking, click —*

Her father's faraway gaze was suddenly bewildered, no longer at the Easter Road stadium but not yet back in his own sitting-room, and with his cup of tea arrested just a few inches from his lips . . .

Not a word. Not a movement. The pair of them freeze-framed in shock. The radio commentary continued: *Ormond's crossed high into the box, Turnbull's there and Laurie Reilly . . .*

She crossed the room to take up position on the fireside rug.

'Hello.' She didn't smile. Didn't step forward to hold out her hand. Didn't make as if she was about to embrace them.

In her unbuttoned coat with the belt hanging loose, she looked like someone who'd just stepped in for a flying visit, someone with a life of their own outside the confines of home and family, someone who decided for herself when she'd arrive and when she'd leave.

She glanced at each of them in turn.

The crowd was cheering, chanting, there was the whirring-ratchet clatter of football rattles.

Her mother? A deeper sag to her shoulders and to her mouth.

Her father? His eyes refusing to meet hers, the fingers of his left hand picking at the armrest of his chair, his half-raised cup of tea now in real danger of spilling. His unaccustomed awkwardness, his uncertainty. His gathering anger.

This was not the man who'd pushed her in the Victoria Park swings every Saturday morning, always so careful to use both hands to keep her safe, taking a step backwards and hauling the wooden seat up to his fullest stretch. 'Higher, Daddy! Higher!' She'd squealed with pleasure as he sent her hurtling forward, her back arched and legs thrust out in front. Arcing upwards and upwards, soaring into the open sky . . .

Her father: 'That's them ahead now, Muriel, 3-2.'

Her mother: *click, clickety-click, clickety-click* . . . (tugging at the length of wool to release a few more coils from the ball at her feet). 'Who's playing again?'

'The Hibees, of course. Against Third Lanark. The Thirds drew with Rangers last season – one more goal and they'd have won us the League for the second year running. But this is just a friendly.'

'Are they not always friendly?'

'Ach, Muriel, you need to take more interest.'

She stepped forward until she was almost touching the knitting needles.

'It's me, Mother.'

Without seeming to notice her own daughter standing in front of her, the older woman turned away and stooped to unhank her line of wool from where the ball had rolled under her seat. That done, she resumed knitting, keeping her head bent over her needles like a conscientious schoolgirl learning a new pattern. Fingering the individual stitches along the length of the needle, she counted them out under her breath. *Eight, nine, ten . . .*

Maggie stared down at the uneven parting in the grey hair, a near-white dandruff-flecked line. As a little girl, she used to watch her mother check her appearance every morning in the hall mirror. Such grown-up neatness was part of an adult world she herself looked forward to belonging to one day. After a last few dabs of face powder the small puff-pad would be replaced in its sleek round tin with the mirror set inside the lid, then, returning to the large oval looking-glass, her mother would angle her head this way and that to check herself first in profile and then full on. Chin on chest and comb in hand, she'd lean forward to inspect the top of her head and smooth out any remaining loose strands, laying them to the right or left of her precisely combed parting.

'But no one sees through your hat, Mum,' Maggie had said to her once.

God does, little one – and so do other women.

The parting she could see now, unprotected either by a hat or stray curls, jerked in abrupt lunges across the exposed skin like a piece of badly done stitchwork, a clumsy suturing of the thinning scalp. Her mother seemed suddenly *much* older. Her father too. As if they'd been fast-forwarded from their mid-fifties straight into premature old age, missing out the years in between.

'Mum?' It was all she could do to stop herself placing a hand on her mother's head and letting it rest there.

'But then I'd no want you ever coming along tae an actual game, Muriel. Fitba terraces are no place for a woman. Nae toilets for a start, less ye fancy joining us in the line, splashing up against the wall!'

'Colin! How can you? Really, you are the very limit sometimes.'

Her mother's shoulders had started to tremble. The light grey knitwork shook in her hands like an unfinished sail billowing in a sea-breeze, except there was no wind and no sailing boat – only an old woman's distress.

'I'm standing here, Mother. Right in front of you.' How hard it was to resist reaching down to take the hands that had begun to shake, to force them to lay aside their knitting; and to make her mother look at her.

Her father got to his feet, crossed over to the radio and turned up the volume:

. . . CAN HOLD THEIR LEAD FOR THE LAST TWO MINUTES. WHAT A FRONT LINE. THE FAMOUS FIVE THEY'VE STARTED CALLING THEM. SMITH, JOHNSTONE, REILLY . . .

Almost cringing under the too-loud commentary now booming around the room, her mother seemed to shrink in her seat, dwindling further into old age.

Her father sat down again.

THE HIBS SUPPORTERS CAN HARDLY BELIEVE WHAT'S HAPPENED. KEEP THIS UP AND NEXT YEAR THE LEAGUE AND CUP DOUBLE MIGHT . . .

She faced each of them in turn: 'Mother? Father?'

. . . THE FAMOUS FIVE LEADING THE MARCH TO VICTORY. THE WHOLE OF EASTER ROAD'S YELLING FOR THE REFEREE TO BLOW HIS . . .

Clenching her hands at her sides, gritting her teeth.

Wanting to march across to the radio and switch it off.

Wanting to rip the knitting out of her mother's hands and yell: LOOK AT ME. MOTHER! LOOK AT ME!

Wanting to pick up her father's tea from the small side-table and throw it in his face . . .

Upstairs, her bedroom was in near-darkness, the curtains pulled shut. No pictures on the walls. No books on the shelves. The mattress stripped. Empty fire grate. Cleared of all her orna-ments and knicknacks, her dressing table had been polished to a hard shine. When she opened the wardrobe, the hangers made a wooden-sounding *clack* as they knocked against each other.

As a teenager she'd taken to tilting the dressing-table mirror this way and that, when checking her appearance. The instant she saw a hint of attractiveness in the sweep of her hair, in her practised smile and the elegance of her unclenched hands, she'd been ready to leave. Where else could she have found the courage to go out and face the world?

And *now*?

Was this really *her* reflection? There was no courage here, nor any sign of it – not in these wounded eyes, these clumsy hands, this slack hair.

Come on, Maggie, come on, she urged the woman in the mirror.

Like the room itself, had she, too, been emptied out,

stripped bare? Her reflection half-raised a hand as if about to offer comfort, only to let it drop again. Then it clenched a fist, clenched and clenched until Maggie felt the fingernails digging into her palms.

Her parents. Her own parents. Within minutes of her confessing what had happened to her, they'd told her to leave the house and never come back. They'd shouted at her and yelled. When she collapsed weeping on the couch, they'd simply got up and walked out the room. Later, in the hall, she'd found her suitcase packed and waiting. They'd ordered her to go, to go now. Pushed her into the vestibule. Pushed and pushed her onto the front step, onto the street. Locked the front door.

She glared at the woman in the mirror – why hadn't she made a scene? Why hadn't she rung the bell, punched and kicked the door? Screamed abuse at them?

Her voice hardly above a whisper but charged with cold, cold fury: how could she have let herself be treated like that? Her whole life . . . like she'd never been born? She heard herself curse the house, curse it to a bombed-out rubble of shattered doorways and gaping windows. Curse her parents trapped in the shut-in self-righteousness of their sitting room.

Clump-clump-clumping back down the stairs as loudly as she could. *Clump-clump-CLUMP!* Maggie came to a stop in the hall. Hesitating. The sitting-room door had been closed again – their chilling contempt beginning to freeze around her.

Behind her, the grandfather clock's relentless *tick . . . tick . . . tick . . .* continued to fill the house. *Tick . . . tick . . . tick . . .* measuring out endurance to the lifeless furniture, to the carpets, doors, corridors, the staircase . . . and to her parents barricaded behind their silence.

Then, and without stopping to think what she was doing, she went straight up to the grandfather clock and its hateful *tick . . . tick . . . tick . . .*

She opened its front case.

She reached in.

TICK . . . TICK . . . TICK . . . TI —

No one paid any attention as Maggie laboured across to the very edge of Newhaven harbour. No one glanced over to see her stand her suitcase on the quayside, then pause for a moment, taking time to gaze down into the sunlit water that rippled-and-broke, rippled-and-broke almost soundlessly against the thick wooden posts.

No one watched her as she pulled back her arm, took aim – then hurled the pendulum as far and as high as she possibly could. Up into the air it rose, glittering as it arced briefly in the afternoon sun, suspended motionless for an instant before falling straight down into the blue-green depths.

There was hardly a splash.

A wonderful moment, and Maggie savoured it. She gave herself a really big smile. As she stood there on the quayside she imagined the dead stillness now filling her parents' house, and pictured the pendulum sinking ever more deeply into the harbour's muddy ooze, its hateful *tick . . . tick . . . tick . . .* choked at last to a permanent silence.

She returned to Princes Street, getting off at the stop between the Scott Monument and the Galleries. It took her so long to pull her suitcase out from below the stairs that she had to struggle through the press of passengers already crowding to get on:

'Out the way, please . . . Please, I'm trying to get off . . . Out of the way . . .'

Then she was down. Once off the tram her suitcase seemed suddenly much heavier than before and she could manage only the clumsiest stumble-steps. Having reached the end of the platform she hesitated, not daring to leave the safety of the tram stop, the one small island of calm in the middle of the rushing street. The city centre was crowded, every department store and shop sure to be packed. Jenners, Fraser's, J&R Allen's, Patrick Thomson's, British Home Stores – the Saturday afternoon shoppers seemed to have melded together into one sweltering mass of summer frocks, hats, handbags, shopping bags and children squeezing in and out of doorways, jostling on the pavements, cramming themselves even more tightly together at junctions while waiting to cross.

The ground beneath shook with the rumble of tram after tram; overhead cables sparked their electric hiss-and-spit; bells dinged warnings to the men and women swarming across the rails. The heat was pounding at her. A few minutes to pull herself together and she'd be all right. Maybe a rest on one of the benches along the stretch of pavement in front of Princes Street Gardens?

Yes.

Gripping her suitcase even tighter, she stepped down onto the street – only to stumble almost at once on the cobbles, and nearly fall.

It was unbearable in the full sun, dizzying almost. Sweat trickled into her eyes and down the side of her face. She wiped it clear. Her blouse stuck to her back. An awkward dash across the tramlines . . .

The first bench was taken. So was the next. And the next.

Lifting and placing each foot . . .

Breathing in, then breathing out . . .

Wiping the sweat from her eyes. Wiping again and again.

All but dragging her suitcase along . . . its arm-wrenching heaviness . . . thump, thump onto the pavement every few steps . . .

Somewhere out of the sun. Somewhere to sit down. Mackie's was too far. Jenners Tearoom? Once inside the store she'd be able to take the lift all the way up to the top floor.

Only, it would mean crossing Princes Street again. It would mean trekking over the uneven cobbles, picking a safe path between lumbering trams that came in both directions. She'd have to struggle through more pedestrians, keep her balance on the shuddering tangle of tram lines that twisted and turned as they caught at her heels.

A few minutes' rest, nothing more.

Then she'd be fine.

Dashing across the front of a stationary tram, and behind another one heading in the opposite direction towards Calton Hill. A van hooted at her, but she paid no attention.

She stepped up onto the pavement. Jenners, at last. The large shop window glared back at her, a harsh cascade of blinding sunlight and raw colours—

Pressing her forehead against the pane of sun-heated glass. Counting to twenty, slowly. Then counting again. Not until she felt she was again standing on solid ground did she continue her journey. The entrance was several yards ahead.

Stepping onto the next paving stone, and the next . . .

She had a special compass trembling and swaying inside

her, of course. Doing its best to guide her. One more step, one more . . .

By the time she managed to stagger out of the sun and into Jenners doorway, it was all she could do to lean against the wall for a moment.

The red-brown marble felt so deliciously cool against her back, the solid stone taking the weight of her exhaustion.

Sweat was now streaming down her face, her neck, her back. Noise clamour brakes horns voices people people people. Surging in and out the doorway, shopping bags knocking against her, feet stumbling against hers, against her suitcase. Knocking it over. 'They'll have it in here . . . said we'd meet at four . . . and some linen for the . . .' Faces staring into hers: 'Are you all right, missus?'

So many rips in the near-transparent curtain that's fallen between her and the city she's known all her life.

People people hectic sky staring sun dizzying blue . . .

A hot wind, such a hot rushing wind springing up out of nowhere, tearing the blameless sky to shreds. Too sudden voices. Too abrupt laughter. Everything too close. Then too far away. The street rushing again rushing again rushing again . . . The hot wind wrenching the arched stonework above, the marbled pillars buckling first to one side, then to the other . . .

The air already sucked out of the next moment and the next . . .

When Maggie opened her eyes, she found she was lying in Jenners' doorway, a man's shiny black shoes planted firmly on the ground right beside her cheek. Strangers brought to a standstill were gazing down at her. Over their shoulders she could see the top of the Scott Monument set against a calmness of sky.

'White as a sheet, the poor woman.'

'Some water, someone.'

One of the faces leant closer, becoming a patch of shadow shielding her from the sun's glare, asking if she was all right?

Did she want to sit up, maybe?

Someone had taken her shoulder.

No. No. No, she screamed back at them, but couldn't make the words come out, not even a whisper.

Asking if she wanted to put her head back, to lean against the wall?

No. No. No.

Asking if she wanted to come inside where there was a chair?

No. No. No.

Someone took her arm and began helping her to her feet.

NO. NO. NO.

If only she could shout the words out loud. If only the people could hear her. If only she could remain peacefully stretched out on the floor of Jenners marbled entrance. Resting there, resting as on layer upon layer of the earth itself – each layer in turn bearing her weight and giving her the peace she longed for and wished could go on for ever.

Meanwhile she'd been helped into the shop . . . helped into a heavily upholstered chair . . . a glass tumbler rattled against her teeth . . . water dribbled down her chin.

'Take your time.' Such kindness in the man's voice, such concern – she could hardly hold back her tears. A woman had placed an arm around her shoulders.

'You'll be all right in a few minutes, lass.'

64

The gentlest squeeze. 'Right as rain.' Another squeeze. A smile. 'If you've a phone at home we can call someone. Your husband, maybe?'

She jerked into sitting upright.

'No phone in the house. I'll be fine. Just the heat.' She tried to smile. She didn't want the woman to withdraw her arm, not yet. So, so comforting even if only for a few more minutes.

'You're a bit peely-wally though. Maybe coming down with—'

'You're very kind. Both of you.'

'Should be at home, feet up, with a magazine, the radio on and him bringing you tea and cake.'

Around her, the noise had quickly built up until it was the same Saturday pell-mell rush all over again. Men and women, their bags and their children, pushing to get in, pushing to get out, pushing to reach the counters, the ringing tills.

She was helped out of the chair. 'Thank you.'

Shaky, but standing. She'd survived the fainting. She'd survived the kindness.

'My man's at the football and—'

She told them she'd be getting a tram home. It wasn't far. Just down to Newhaven. She'd be fine now. Totally fine. Really.

'Well, if you're sure you're okay, lass . . . ?'

As steadily as she could, she walked out of the department store and back into the glare of Princes Street, setting off in the direction of the tram stop opposite Waverley Steps.

Then a miracle happened.

'MAGGIE!'

Getting a tram home? She had no home. She kept walking.

When she reached the stop – what then? *Somewhere to stay Somewhere to stay Somewhere to stay . . .*

'MAGGIE!'

She looked round. Bleach-bottle blonde, pillar-box red lipstick, cheerful and friendly. It was her sister-in-law.

The older woman stood directly in front of her: 'Remember me?' She was joking, of course.

'Oh, Jean! Hello there. I'm – I'm—'

Jean glanced down at the suitcase: 'Are you coming, or going?'

'I don't know.'

The two women looked at each other.

'It's true, Jean. I really don't know if I'm coming or going!'

Which made them both laugh out loud.

Ten minutes later Maggie was being treated to afternoon tea at the North British. Busy restaurant, chattering on all sides, waitresses in black starched uniforms, comfortable seat, a two-tiered cake stand – scones at the bottom and an upper layer of fancy cakes. There was a dish of glistening wet-yellow pats of butter, three kinds of jam, honey and clotted cream. No ration problems here. Two pots – one for tea, one for hot water. Linen napkins.

Her sister-in-law had her own small business as a quality baker, making cakes and confectionery to order. Not until some years later, when Jean could finally afford to give up the rented one-room flat where she did her baking and lease proper shop premises in Haymarket – practically the West End, after all – was her professional status finally acknowledged by her mother-in-law. Until then she was always referred to as Jean,

Billy's wife, who does us a nice cake when the pair of them come round. Her hair was too blonde, her lips too red and her accent . . . too *Dalry.*

'Another brandy snap? Some cake? Let's hope it's just twae yer eating fer!' Jean nodded towards the few remaining crumbs on Maggie's empty plate.

'Wonderful to see you again, Jean. You've no idea.'

Her sister-in-law smiled. 'Feeling mair like yersel, are ye?'

'Yes, thank you. A bit shaky back there with the heat and—'

'Billy telt me whit happened. Ye poor woman! Throwing their ain daughter oot on the street. I'm scunnered, fair scunnered! Whit a shameless pair o—'

'It's my own fault, Jean. If I hadn't let myself be—'

'Dinna talk daft. That's the wey men talk, but we ken better. See, Maggie—'

'I feel so – so *ashamed*. When he drove me back home – *afterwards*, you understand? – he hardly spoke a word, just dropped me at the end of my street,' she paused. 'After all his talk and his promises, suddenly I was nothing. That look on his face as he drove off . . . A smile right enough, but like he was glad to be rid of me . . . So much dirt he'd scraped off his—'

'Maggie, dinna let yersel—!'

'Could feel the shame of it burning into me as I went up our front steps.'

'But, Maggie, ye shouldnae feel—'

'Let me say it, Jean. I've not talked with anyone. Once I knew I was . . . well, you know what I mean . . . Anyway, when I tried to tell Mum and Dad . . . they were even worse. Their disgust, like I was the lowest of the low. I went to the YW that night and—'

'Ye should've cam tae me. I'd hiv—'

'I couldn't bear to see anyone. I wanted to be where no one knew me. Next morning I went to Lewis.'

'Whit?' Jean's cry of surprise silenced the nearby tables. She continued in a low voice, 'Lewis? What in God's name possessed ye tae fetch yersel there?'

Maggie shrugged. 'Relatives, but I didn't know them, never even met them before, and so I thought everything would be—' She shook her head. 'Truth is, I wasn't thinking straight. I should've written to them first and saved myself the trip.' Managing not to cry, she told her sister-in-law about the hundred thousand welcomes she'd received.

Long before she was finished, Jean's hand had reached across to cover hers. 'I tell ye, Maggie, I hope thae Callanders burn in Hell.'

'That's an awful thing to say.'

The older woman shrugged and took out a packet of cigarettes. 'Smoke?'

'No thanks.'

Jean lit up. 'Some family you're frae! Even my Billy – and he's the best of thon heartless brood – willnae want tae hear we've met. So I'll no be telling him.' She took a draw of her cigarette. 'Yer gang ahead wi it then?'

'I suppose so.'

'Hmm.' She paused to tap off some ash. 'Well, I'm glad tae hear yer no thinking o some back street butcher or of daein it yersel wi gin and knitting needles.'

Maggie had managed to put away two slices of chocolate

sponge, a nut-tasting cake with yellow icing and two scones with butter and strawberry jam. Feeling so much better than earlier, she licked the tip of her forefinger and dabbed at the cake crumbs.

'Which reminds me, Maggie, when yer time comes, promise me ye'll no be seeking refuge in the airms o Christ?'

'What?'

'Promise me you'll book intae a proper nursing home. Promise me, Maggie. You're no gang tae be yin o those poor women doun on their hands and knees scrubbing the church flagstones right up tae the last minute, then getting tied tae a table tae gie birth. I've heard some awfae stories. We're no having merciful sisters saying you and yer sinful bairn are gang straight tae hell and gien ye both a taste of damnation in advance. We're no letting that happen. How are ye fer money, by the bye?'

'Fine for the moment. Something in the Post Office.'

'Good. And where are ye biding?'

'Back at the YW, I suppose.'

'Well, I know a place – *in darkest, slummiest Dalry,*' Jean said, imitating her mother-in-law's put-on posh. 'It'll dae fer the time being. All right?'

'Jean, I can't—'

'Not good enough fer you?'

'No, I don't mean—'

'That's that sorted then. And . . . the man?'

Maggie shrugged. What was there to say?

Jean ground out her half-smoked cigarette. 'He can burn as weel.'

§

Jean's small bakery turned out to be an Aladdin's cave just off the Dalry Road. Maggie stepped from the grim, cobbled side street of stone-faced tenements straight into a one-room oriental palace where the oven-warm air was drenched with the scents of cinnamon, cinnabar and cloves, with the sweetness of melted chocolate and icing sugar. Like King and Queen, a large gas cooker and a generously deep kitchen sink ruled over an assembled court of shelf upon shelf of flour tins, spice racks, glass jars of raisins, currants, almonds, dried orange and lemon peel . . .

'I'm a black-market baker,' she joked, 'either that or I'd be stuck daein scones and naethin but!'

The sitting room/kitchen of Jean's small 'single end' flat was for her baking work only, but she'd fitted up the snug, cabin-sized boxroom at the back as a restroom, should she ever feel like putting her feet up. Instead of a bed there was the luxury of a Louis-the-Something chaise longue. Some blankets and a spare cushion were kept in a small trunk whose flat lid doubled as a side table. For Maggie, it was perfect.

Once Jean had left to go home, promising to be back first thing Monday morning, Maggie got herself settled in. A few days? A few weeks? She'd no idea, but for the time being this would be home. Her coat and scarf she hung on the back of the boxroom door, her best dress on a coat hanger that was nailed to the wall, creating a pleasing splash of blue and green against the pale-coloured wallpaper. Her two blouses went on another hanger to decorate the wall opposite. The rest of her clothes – a cardigan, two skirts, a jersey, her underwear and stockings – remained in her suitcase which she stowed under the couch. The chaise longue had gilt arm- and back-rests, and was upholstered in thick red velvet. Its remaining three legs were slender and curved gracefully upwards suggesting effortless, indeed miraculous, support; the fourth had been replaced by a weight from an old set of grocer's scales. The couch felt quite solid and secure, however. All in all, there was a certain elegance to her new sleeping arrangements, Maggie decided – and she intended to do her best to live up to it.

That evening as she shook out the first blanket, she heard her mother's voice: *You've made your bed, now you have to lie on it.*

'I will,' she heard herself reply out loud, 'just watch me!'

Two days later Maggie saw the handwritten notice in the window of Fusco's Fish Restaurant on Gorgie Road, and went straight in. Perfect timing. She could hardly believe her luck – the usual assistant had just been sacked after turning up drunk and two hours late, yet again. If she could start at once, the job was hers – six-day week serving from 11 to 8, with two hours off in the afternoon. Haddock and chips, cod and chips, white pudding supper, black pudding supper, sausage and chips, steak pie and chips. Pickled eggs, pickled onions. At least she'd never go hungry. Tony Fusco had been an Italian POW who'd stayed on in Scotland and ended up marrying a girl from Leith.

'She called Maggie like you! Good name, good woman – you work good, too!'

Her nylon overalls were several sizes too big, which was a real plus as they'd help keep her 'situation' hidden for a good while longer. The Light Programme coming from the

shelf above the till helped the minutes pass, if not the hours –
*Music While You Work, Housewives' Choice, Workers' Play-
time* . . . By the end of her first evening, the hours had slowed
down to a crawl and she was so tired that she could hardly
stop the chips from leaping off her scoop before they reached
the newspaper, or the fish from nose-diving onto the floor as
she carried the plates through to the sit-ins. Already she was
looking forward to her first Sunday off – she'd stay in bed and
enjoy a double-shift of deep-fried sleep.

Grace, who worked at Fusco's from five in the afternoon
till it closed at eleven, had helped her get started: 'Think of yer
man and ram yer fish in the fryer fer a richt guid battering!'
Slow Peter worked in the kitchen; he hardly spoke but instead
offered the world a permanent grin.

A few days after she'd started, Maggie happened to
mention she was looking for a place to stay.

'Yer in luck!' Grace grinned at her. 'Mrs McKenzie's
lodger frae across oor landing, a widow woman, passed away
last night. The room'll be going spare. If ye want, I'll let Mrs
M ken you're interested. Ye can look in afore work the morn.
If ye dinnae fancy it, no harm done. The auld soul'll be getting
carried out first thing so ye can get yersel moved straight in,
same day. I'm sure Tony'll let you off for a bit longer in the
afternoon to get things sorted. A whole room tae yersel – I'm
jealous already!'

When Maggie called round after ten the following
morning, Mrs McKenzie apologised, saying the undertakers
hadn't turned up yet, but now that she was here Maggie might
as well take a look round. 'Dinna fear – she's decent.'

They went into the room. Not only was it much larger

than her boxroom at Jean's, but there was a window, and a door that she could lock. Perfect.

Mrs McKenzie nodded in the direction of the sheet-covered figure stretched out on the bed. 'She'll be out by this evening, Miss Davies.' Then, pointing to the gas meter beside the fire, she added, 'Ye canna say Isa was tight-fisted – she's left ye a good shilling's worth!'

Having discussed terms, Maggie agreed to come back with her suitcase during her afternoon break, and move in properly after work.

When she returned at eight-thirty that evening the room was all hers. The dead woman's bed stood in the corner. Opposite was a family-sized tombstone of a wardrobe that reeked of shoes, old clothes and camphor. The top of the dresser was a clutter of postcards, photographs, some letters in a rack, a comb, nailfile, a *Present from Dunbar* ashtray; wisps of greyish hair were tangled among the bristles of the hairbrush.

Maggie dumped the lot into an old tartan shopping bag she found hanging behind the door, to go out in the next bin collection. She felt sad for the widow woman dying here alone, but the less she knew about her the better she'd get on. The drawers were empty. Mrs McKenzie must have gone through them already.

She set about making the bed. A Louis-the-Something chaise longue was one thing, but a real bed with a mattress, clean-smelling sheets, thick blankets and a quilt that fitted neat as a pie-crust on top was quite another matter. After a full day on her feet, scooping and salting, she could hardly wait to climb in under that welcoming crust and get baked to sleep. She had a quick wash in the bathroom down the hall, undressed and got under the blankets. So snug and pie-warm!

It was only when she laid her head on the pillow that she realised she'd just made her bed without hearing her mother's usual comment. She grinned to herself in the dark. It was a good start.

For the next three months Maggie would sleepwalk out from her room at Mrs McKenzie's, down the stairs, along Fountainbridge, over the railway, past the graveyard, then sharp right, down to the junction, across to the start of Gorgie Road, under a railway bridge and straight on till she reached Fusco's – and sleepwalk back again nine hours later. Back and forth, back and forth, six times a week, like she was in a dream. Someone else's dream, not hers.

Every Saturday evening she went to Mrs Mackenzie's kitchen to pay her week's rent in advance, placing the ten-shilling note and loose coins onto her landlady's waiting palm. Back in her room she dropped whatever cash remained, uncounted, into the empty drawer of her bedside cabinet to join the previous weeks' earnings and the slither of pennies, threepenny bits, and occasional sixpences she'd been given as tips. If she needed to buy something, she took a handful of small change from the drawer. She spent very little. With Sunday as her only day off, she didn't have much opportunity – all the shops were shut and so were the cinemas and variety shows. She was at liberty to go to church, of course. Failing that, she was free to walk up and down the more or less deserted streets, or, if she found a park that was unlocked, she could stroll along the paths, past playgrounds with their swings, roundabouts and the witch's hat all chained up for the Sabbath. There was no question of visiting her brother Billy at home. It would be like visiting her parents all over again – except it'd make things really hard for her sister-in-law.

The best Sundays were when there was a light in Jean's shop, which meant she was having to work over the weekend. What a joy it was to walk into the comforting smell of cakes and baking, the sweetness of thick icing and melting chocolate, and the luxury of her sister-in-law's good humour and kindness. Here Maggie would sit and chat, and laugh, and tell Fusco stories about some of her customers, about Grace and her football-daft husband Norrie, storing up Jean's cheerfulness inside her to carry back to her room at Mrs McKenzie's.

'Were you ever in the Hebrides?'

Without glancing up, Maggie continued scooping chips into the newspaper. 'Salt and sauce?'

'The both, please. I'm wondering, were you ever in the Hebrides, on Lewis?'

She shook on the salt, then the sauce. 'Pickled onion?'

'No thanks. Stornoway maybe? Can ye double-wrap? I'll be taking them back to the B&B.'

'No, never been.' Maggie finished folding the two extra sheets of newspaper around the fish supper. Now she'd have to hand it over, to raise her eyes and look at the customer.

He was early thirties, red hair. Never seen him before. She took the man's half-crown and rang up the till.

'Didn't you stay at Mrs Stewart's boarding house a few months back?'

Her hand shook as she laid out the man's change on the counter.

'Stewart? I don't know anybody called Stewart. Never been to Lewis either, like I said.' But even as she spoke she could feel herself blush. She drew her hand across her face as if to wipe away sweat. It suddenly seemed hotter than ever standing next to the fryer.

'You've a perfect double then – Michael showed me a photograph. Not that he can see it, poor man, but he keeps it.'

When Maggie made no reply, he continued. 'Well, maybe I'm wrong, but I'll give him your best. *Greetings from a bonnie lass in Edinburgh! Michael'd* like that!' A moment later the man was gone.

For the rest of that shift, Maggie let her hands carry on with the scooping, salting and wrapping while she herself stood again at the window of her room at Mrs Stewart's gazing out over the harbour, Michael's arms around her.

A week later she came into the chip shop to find Grace grinning from ear to ear.

'Ye've got fan mail!' Grace pointed to an envelope propped on the shelf next to the radio. 'Came this morning, Tony says.'

Margaret Davies, c/o Fusco's Fish Restaurant, Gorgie Road, Edinburgh. Firm handwriting, neat fountain pen.

'Postmarked Stornoway. Whae'd ye ken in thon place?'

Maggie stuck it in the pocket of her overalls. 'Relatives.'

'In the land o the Wee Frees?'

A second letter came in the afternoon post.

'Mair relatives?' asked Grace.

Back at Mrs McKenzie's, her coat still on, she sat on the

edge of her bed and tore open the first envelope. She unfolded the light blue notepaper –

Dearest Maggie, . . . I still think of it as your room, as our room really after all we shared together there . . . When I came downstairs in the morning to find you . . .

But she was hardly able to read the words, as written down by his friend Lachlan. Her tears seemed to have come from nowhere.

She wrote back to Michael an hour later.

It was the last Saturday in August. Since starting at eleven that morning she'd been scooping and salting for three hours solid while walking miles, it felt like, up and down the same stretch of lino behind the metal counter. The occasional trip to the back kitchen or to carry heaped plates into the side room had seemed like a relief. Her face, the inside of her mouth and even her lungs felt so clotted with grease that, by the time the lunch customers left, she felt she herself had been battered and basted to a turn. Forget staying indoors. She went out onto the back green. Putting her plate on the step, she eased herself down onto the sun-warmed stone and leant against the tenement wall. She slipped off her shoes. At last she could relax completely. Balancing her steak pie and chips on her knees, and with a cup of sweetened tea to hand, she was to all appearances a woman without a care in the world. Thanks to the loose-fitting overalls no one could notice that she was starting to show. She ate slowly while staring at the sheets and pillowcases, shirts, dresses and underwear strung out on the drying lines.

'Maggie?'

Tony was standing in the doorway. She put down her fork.

'Hi, Tony.'

'Grace, she very tired. Like dog she say. Good you got more sense than have babies, Maggie. You stay more late this night, help me? Much peoples. I do money, you chips – easy.'

Grace, too, was pregnant. During the slack periods Maggie was kept up to date with the expectant mother's state of health, her ever-changing views on baby clothes and baby care. The younger woman had slept well the previous night, or not so well. The baby had kicked. The baby had kicked again. Did Maggie think a newborn should be left to cry like that scientist said on the radio or picked up at once? Grace didn't want to spoil him. A girl was different. But it was going to be a boy because that's what Norrie wanted – someone to play for the Hearts. Should he be bottle- or breast-fed? She talked about cribs, prams, grandparents; she detailed how she coped with morning sickness, exhaustion, swollen ankles. Maggie was spared none of it and endured every last symptom and circumstance while unable to say anything of her own in return. Sometimes she felt like screaming.

'Happy to help, Tony.' It would get her through another day.

'Thanks, thanks. Real big help for me. For Grace too. For you extra money.'

'Always welcome.' Maggie waved her fork to show how pleased she was.

'More tips when pubs shut. Saturday night is different peoples. But I always here and Slow Peter. So no worry, Maggie.'

§

Dressed in his usual blue overalls and sandshoes without socks, Slow Peter was standing at the kitchen sink with his back to her, rinsing dishes. It was eight o'clock. The weather had broken and for the last half hour heavy rain had been battering the kitchen window.

She watched him run water over one side of a plate, turn it over, then rinse the other. Careful and methodical, he filled slot after slot on the drying rack. One plate . . . one plate . . . one plate. She sighed as she put down the fresh stack of dirty dishes she'd brought through.

'You fine, Maggie?'

'Fine, thanks, Peter. Bit tired.'

Slow Peter lifted the top plate and began scraping the leftovers, some fish batter and mashed-up chips, into the metal waste bin next to his sink. It was a badly dented oil drum with *Mobil* lettered in red.

'Pigs'll be grinning the night. Like Christmas dinner tae them.'

That rancid smell of fried fat – she'd need to wash it out of her hair before she could finally crawl into bed. She'd put on fresh sheets before leaving for work to be ready for tomorrow's all-day sleep. Would there be any hot water left? Had she a clean towel? Nearly three hours to go, more like three years.

'*My* pigs is always pleased tae see me. Smiling and grinning they are. Cleans their bowls tae the last lick, not like *them*.' He jerked his head in the direction of the side room while tipping an uneaten fish cake into his drum.

Maggie smiled, not a waitress-smile this time but the real thing.

'We were taught to never waste food.' The instant she

spoke she realised she was sounding like her mother, but couldn't seem to stop: 'Rationing, you understand, and the War. My mother . . .' she heard herself blundering on, 'she made soup out of anything. Even the cheese rinds went in. And bones too, of course.'

'*My* pigs eats bones.'

'We didn't actually eat the bones, Peter.' Her mother's voice again, her mother sitting in the Newhaven house, her knitting needles endlessly *click-clicking, click-clicking, click-clicking* . . .

'You sure you're okay, Maggie?' Slow Peter was holding out a soapy wet hand as if offering to steady her.

Thirty-one years old, and over six months pregnant. No husband. No family. Spending her Saturday night standing in puddles of greasy kitchen water in the back room of a rain-lashed fish and chip shop on Gorgie Road – she was okay?

'Fine thanks.'

What else could she say to a *man*? Even to kindly Slow Peter? If she clammed up, if she did her best to ignore him, to ignore them all, there they'd still be, as always, the men of this world – like so many closed doors blocking her at every turn. Unless, of course, they wanted something enough to let her in. Afterwards the door was slammed shut . . . and she'd be shoved out into the street once more. Always the same closed door, the same street, the same man-made world. Not Michael, though, and his letters of long-distance affection . . . the words and phrases repeated over and over . . . hope . . . happiness . . . one day . . . you and me . . . They helped her blot out everything else. The photograph he'd sent her of him in his uniform stood propped up on her bedside table like a souvenir of another life, someone else's. Often, when she was about to write to him, she'd sit on the edge of her bed and let her fingertip trace the forehead, the cheeks and lips she could see in the photograph, like he'd shown her. No white stick, no milky eyes – but, yes, it *was* Michael, *her* Michael. Of course it was. And she loved him.

'I'm fine, Peter. Thanks.' Another half-smile, a waitress one this time. 'Better get back through.'

'Bye, bye, Maggie.'

She returned to find a queue had built up – a line of pig snouts and trotters at their counter-long feeding trough. Cod and chips no sauce – scoop and scoop, salt and wrap / pie supper with two pickled onions – scoop and scoop, salt and sauce and wrap / three sit-in suppers for a family guzzling at their own small trough in the side room. Back to the queue . . .

They started piling in at closing time. Piling in, staggering in, tumbling in, falling in, laughing, singing, joking, flirting; the queue soon became a multi-headed beast with no tail in sight. Some were drunk, some very drunk. Loud and cheerful, mostly. Tony had said to her, 'Like in pub – they at counter, they get served.'

By ten-thirty she was worn out, utterly.

At last the queue had dwindled to nothing and the counter was deserted except for a solitary man at the far end in drenched-through overalls, finishing his sixpenny bag. He stood, dripped and fed one chip after another into his mouth while staring out at the darkening street. He'd be leaving any minute. That was the good news. The bad news was that Norrie had turned up. Norrie was Grace's husband. Drunk but still on his feet, he'd come roistering in at closing time with some other men to mop up the night's beer with sit-in suppers all-round. The three men were in their thirties and heavily built. One wearing his cap with the brim pulled down low like a duck-bill, another with fair hair and a hesitant moustache. Norrie, in a blue check shirt, had his work jacket slung over the chair back. It seemed they'd just been paid off from building work on some new bungalows up the road. They seemed to fill the cafe with their noise.

She leant against the counter, giving the stainless steel a last wipe with a wet cloth.

'A seat here for ye, Maggie. Rab's been keeping it warm for ye!' Norrie looked flushed with drink. 'He's eaten good and's fair raring for his afters!'

Duck Bill roared with laughter, the Moustache gave Norrie a punch on the arm.

She managed a half nod in their direction while sidling herself and her cloth further off down the counter.

'Been a bit pan-loafie, aren't ye, Maggie?' Norrie called out. No need to look over, she could imagine him sticking his nose in the air to mime a mock-polite sniff, and not for the first time.

'Yer no frae Gorgie, are ye? Fancy yersel New Town? Morningside?' Duck Bill chipped in.

'Where *sex* is what their coal gets delivered in!' shouted Norrie. More laughter.

The man in the overalls had now finished his chips and was holding out the scrunched-up wrapping paper for her to take. She was forced to return back along the counter, for the bin.

'Naebody misses a slice off a cut loaf, pan or plain, eh?' The Moustache grinned at her and patted the empty seat beside him.

'Rab's no being cheeky or nowt, Maggie.' Norrie stubbed out his cigarette in his half-finished black pudding supper as he called over to her: 'Sae lang as yer a woman's whit he means. An yer aa that!' Even at that distance his sun-beaten face showed the tiredness of several days' grey stubble.

'Things okey-dokey, Maggie?' Tony had come through from the kitchen and was ringing up the till.

'Fine.' She waitress-smiled and tucked a loose strand of hair behind her ear.

Smell the cooking grease on it? She could *feel* it, a smeary slickness that stuck the separate strands together into a solid, larded hank.

Norrie had started singing:

'Rab kens a lassie, a bonnie, Scottish lassie,

She's sweet as the heather in the dell . . .'

The others joined in, clapping in time.

'There's nane sae classie as Rab's bonnie lassie,

Maggie, his Scots bluebell!'

Loud cheers. Applause. Expectant faces turned in her direction. The windows were steamed up, but she could see the rain coming down harder than ever. The headlights of a passing car swept the darkness. If she was lucky she might still get the last tram home . . .

Back through in the kitchen she ran herself a glass of cold water and dabbed her face and brow.

Slow Peter straightened up from stacking plates in a cupboard. 'These pigs likes their windows closed tight. Gets choking hot.'

'I'm okay now, thanks. Long day.'

'Days here aye long.' Slow Peter picked up more plates. 'Sunday the morn. Shortest of the week, but aye the best.'

'You said it, Peter.' She returned to the counter.

'Here she comes. Rab's bonnie lassie!' called Norrie. 'Maggie, ye broke his hairt when ye went away there! Couldnae even finish his chips – we thocht he wis a goner.'

Another laugh.

'Likely he'll be needing the kiss of life – and yer the only woman in the place. Job's all yours!'

More laughter, hands slapping the table top.

The kiss of life? She'd gone on only one date with the man she'd met at Fairley's – a drive down to Silverknowes in his Morris Minor. A romantic stroll along the seafront, he suggested. They'd parked at the top end away from the streetlights and that's when a sudden downpour started. The heavens emptied. He suggested they move into the back seat *to be more comfortable*. Again . . . and again . . . and again the slow sweep of a lighthouse beam from the island out in the Forth lit up his face, then drew total darkness over it: *I want to show how much I care for you, Maggie. I want to show you. I want so much to –*

'Kiss of life we're saying, Maggie!'

. . . The smell of the leather seats, the heavy rain clattering onto the thin metal roof only inches above her head. The offer of whisky from his hip flask.

No, thanks.

I'm drinking for two then. Cheers.

That peat-brown brackishness on the man's breath, making her pull away. A real stomach-churning –

The memory made her want to gag, to turn away like

she was still trying to avoid the man's lips, to squirm away from his touch. The beam of the lighthouse still searing her eyes . . .

She gripped the metal edge to steady herself, gripped it tight and held on. Doing her best to shut out the men in the cafe, to shut out the cafe itself, the darkness, the wind and rain, to shut out everything. Kiss of life? She wanted Michael's kiss, she wanted his arms around her, holding her safe and secure, shutting out the rest of the world . . .

Without any warning she felt a flutter deep inside her. So faint and seeming to have come from nowhere . . . Like nothing she'd ever . . .

But she knew at once what it was. She recognised it. Had been waiting for it . . .

Making her feel . . .? Making her feel that everything she'd ever known before, ever seen before, touched, heard . . .

She stood quite still, her hands resting on the counter, and suddenly nothing else mattered.

Nothing. Else. Mattered.

Fusco's was empty at last.

'You go now, Maggie. I finish. Good work. Good work.' Tony handed her two half-crowns. 'This for you.'

'Thanks. Like I said, happy to help.' Waitress words, waitress smile. 'Goodnight, Tony.'

She went through to the kitchen for her coat.

Slow Peter must have left. Clean scoops and sieves hung from their hooks on the wall, dishcloths were spread out to dry over taps and racks, the sink and draining board gleamed. She felt she could have lain down on the main worktable there and then, and been asleep within seconds.

Taking her coat out from the broom cupboard, she headed for the street door.

'Good night, Maggie. You safe home now.'

She waved goodbye. 'See you Monday.'

It had stopped raining. Apart from the occasional car, its tyres hissing on the wet cobbles, and the few late-night stragglers making their way home, Gorgie Road was more or less deserted. She hurried along the pavement, side-stepping the puddles and the occasional gush of rainwater from a rone pipe. It was well after eleven o'clock. Fingers crossed there might still be a last tram.

Time to step lively. Past the line of closed shops, past the Tynecastle street-end, quick-marching under the railway bridge, singing to herself to set a good pace: *I love a lassie, a bonnie Scottish lassie . . .*' A very brisk fifteen minutes and she'd be home.

Coming up to the Dalry Road junction. To left and right stretched a darkness of streetlamps spaced further and further apart, straight ahead lay an empty street of closed doors and tenement windows with their curtains pulled. No wind any more, the air damp and everything silent. A few parked cars and hardly a sound except for the brisk *click-click-click* of her heels on the pavement echoing back from the wall.

Sweet as the heather in the dell . . .

Footsteps.

Someone else's, and coming close behind. Long steady strides. A man's.

Starting to speed up: *Nane sae classie-as-ma-bonnie-*

lassie . . .

'Hey there!'

She felt herself freeze inside. Freeze and close up tight.

Then abruptly walking even faster: *A-bonnie-bonnie-lassie* . . .

'Hey there, Maggie, wait a moment!'

It was Norrie, and he'd almost caught up with her.

'What are ye running for? Olympics were last year. Just saying hello. Friendly greeting, Maggie, that's all.' He was now level with her. 'You're yin fast woman right enough!'

She could smell the beer on him. 'That's because I want to get home.'

Keeping her eyes fixed straight ahead, she accelerated to double-speed.

Another flutter, stronger than before . . .

'Couldnae be better! The baith o us gang the same way, being neighbours like, on the same stair. Grand, eh!'

'It's late.'

Fluttering like the very gentlest *kick-kick-kick* . . .

'I'm walking ye back, seeing ye safe home.'

'I'm fine thanks.'

Kick-kick-kick . . . Yes, she was fine – they were *both* fine. Needing nothing except to be left alone.

'Ye dinnae like me?'

'Go away, Norrie. I'm tired. Been on my feet all day and—'

His hand grasping her arm, his fingers digging into her elbow. Making her stop in mid-stride.

'Ye dinna like me?'

'Go away, I'm telling you.' Trying to shake herself free. 'Stop it.'

His grip was too strong. Forcing her to turn and look at him. His face only inches away, his unshaven cheeks looking dingy and raw.

'Let go, you're hurting me.'

'Then say ye like me.'

Squeezing her arm harder.

She gritted her teeth. 'What do you mean – *Say I like you?* What about Grace?'

'Grace isnae here.' Another squeeze. 'Come on.'

So tense now she could hardly manage to speak.

'But Grace'll be waiting for you to come—'

'SAY IT, Maggie.'

'I'm saying nothing. Let go of me.'

'Yer a quiet yin, richt enough. Need encouraging. Am I right?' He passed his hand over her hair, stroking it lightly. 'Shy's right for a lady, ken? A proper lady. Makes them . . . *special*.' Stroking her cheek. 'Makes you special. Let's walk th'gither.'

Forced to walk at his side she remained rigid, her face turned away from him.

A house light clicked off as they came to the beginning of Fountainbridge. Mrs McKenzie's was only five minutes away, five minutes at most.

He paused before crossing the street. 'Rare night, eh, Maggie? All the stars and everything. Peaceful. Like in the black-out. Mind hou bonnie the sky looked then?'

Jerking her elbow, making her stumble forward across the main road before abruptly wheeling her round into a side street. 'No far nou.'

'But this isn't the way to—'

'Shut it, Maggie. Or I'll shut you.' His arm had moved around her shoulder to hold her more firmly.

Like she was resting her head on his shoulder, her face pressed up against the grit and greasiness of his work jacket. To anyone else they'd probably look like a courting couple making their way home – and if she screamed, folk would just think they were having a row . . .

But there was no one to see them. The street was deserted, the tenement windows curtained.

'Grace hisnae let me near her in weeks. She's nae wife tae me. It's bairn this an bairn that.'

'But, Norrie—'

'Shut it, I said.' He marched her another twenty yards. 'Dinna be feart, Maggie. I'm no gang to harm ye. I *like* ye. I really do. Nothing bad's gang tae happen. I promise.'

Into the next street.

'Wanting tae show ye whit I'd done, is aa. Grace isnae interested – just in the money I bring hame. But I'm proud o whit I've done an ken ye'll appreciate it. Ye've got class.' Another squeeze.

A few steps later he halted outside the first in a line of new bungalows.

'Folks'll be moving in Monday.' Hauling her up the steps to the front door. 'I kept us a key.'

SUNDAY

THE WHITEBOARD IN the hall reads TODAY IS . . . MONDAY.

Boss Beryl's come up to you saying, 'What're you doing here, Maggie? Waiting for a bus? Won't come just because you're standing here.'

No point saying anything back to the likes of Boss Beryl, so no one ever does. Complete waste of time.

You mumble what might be a yes or might be a no and give her a shrug, making it look like you're really heading towards the dayroom . . .

But if you really do walk off, then you'll just have to turn and come all the way back once she's gone.

So you rein in your zimmer and give her a puzzled look. Puzzled, and yet hopeful.

'The fact is, Beryl, I'm waiting for a number 26. Maybe you can help me? Do you have any idea when the next one's due? It'll take me right along Princes Street. Pity there's no timetable. Can't Mrs Saunders get one fixed up?'

The look on her torn face! She'll certainly not be hanging around much longer. *She's got better things to do than . . .*

And so . . .

Not even the hint of grin: 'Or, if a 7 turns up I'll ask for a two-penny transfer and get off in Princes Street. Some of the shops stay open over lunchtime and . . .'

Success. Boss Beryl's given a snort, shaken her head and said that she's got better things to do than stand around passing the time of day.

After waiting to make sure she's gone all the way down the corridor and disappeared round the corner, you execute a neat U-turn and zimmer yourself right up to the board. No one about – and so you grab hold of the marker pen . . .

The shaft of sunlight from the bay window has started inching its way across the lino, turning the chairs lined up against the walls into the hour marks scratched on a sundial. Anyone coming in the door can tell what time it is by how far the sun has travelled round the room and who it's pointing at. It's Dorothy o'clock now. The old woman doesn't move a muscle, doesn't even turn away to shield her eyes.

You changed what was written on the whiteboard, of course. Not that you believe today will end up any different because of *that*. You're not that far gone. But TODAY IS . . . SUNDAY written up there for everyone to read, must mean *something*? The words are real words that make real sense, so they can't be completely wrong. They must be a little bit true. Surely?

Here in the dayroom things move forward only when the sun carries them, and at meal times. You come in, take your seat. No one changes their seat or gets up and walks anywhere except on the TV screen where folk are always talking and waving their arms and having car chases with emergency blue lights and sirens and loud crashes. But there's no point trying to follow what's being said or –

'Your son's here, Maggie.'

'Who? Someone's here *today*?'

For a moment it seems that Fred Astaire has appeared in the doorway looking for a new partner to dance with, but without his top hat. After pausing to check who's sitting where, he's come across the empty space in the middle of the room like he's wading through a pool of sunlight, splashing brightness on everyone. He's making straight for you.

You'd like to hold out your arms for him to take you and lift you onto your feet, then together the two of you'll go whirling round and round the dance floor.

'But today's really called Monday.' Damn. You've gone and said it out loud before you could stop yourself. You don't want them to find out it was you who changed the board, do you? Of course not. But you can't have really made it Sunday . . . ?

He's standing in front of you. Will he reach up to touch the side of your face, let his fingertips pass slowly over your eyes and lips?

'Happy Birthday!' His hands on your shoulders, he's bent forward to kiss you on the forehead. The briefest touch and he's already back in his seat. Too quick. All too quick and finished with.

'My birthday?' You can hardly follow what he's saying. Doesn't he want to clasp you in his arms? Pass his hands over your face?

Can he really *see* you?

'Congratulations! Happy Birthday, Mum. Ninety – and looking FABULOUS! That's why I've driven down special to be here today. Didn't they have the cake at lunchtime that I ordered? And everyone singing *Happy Birthday*?'

'Cake? Yes, I remember cake.'

Before you know what's happening, he's waving his hands in the air – making magic passes is what he calls it. A trick – he's doing a magic trick like he says he sometimes does on TV. Maybe he'll make you vanish in a puff of smoke? Or else the Murray twins will start talking? Or else Dorothy? Or . . . ?

There's the flick of a yellow silk handkerchief that he's pulled out of nowhere:

'Let the sun shine and the earth whirl,

For our very own . . . birthday girl!

Happy Birthday, Mum!'

A small package has suddenly appeared on your lap, wrapped in red paper and tied with curly gold ribbon. He's helping you with the ribbon, the paper.

You mutter a thank-you, adding that it's very kind of him. What else can you say?

It's a book. A book with a hard red cover. You never asked for a book. He wouldn't know you stopped reading a long time ago. Sad stories, they always felt sad. All that living that just goes on and on until it tears the heart out of you, till you *ache*.

'For you, Mum. I made it.'

Only there's no title. Nothing written on the front or on the back. No pages even, not the usual kind of pages anyway.

'Well, come on, Mum, open it!'

The first page: A black and white photograph set in a plastic sleeve. Not a book at all, but photographs like in a family album. That's what it is – somebody's photo album. Out of politeness you flick through the opening pages while he tells you he'd come across a lot of photos in an envelope

93

in a cupboard, along with your old typewriter. Halfway through, you stop at a snap of some couple or other posing outside their house –

Complete strangers.

Makes you feel bad seeing them, whoever they are. Makes you feel ashamed, poking your nose into other people's lives. You give him the album back.

But all he does is show you another picture. This time . . . it's you! A photograph of you wearing a starched white blouse and looking very efficient, your hands poised above the keyboard of an ancient-looking typewriter. Your old *Underwood*.

'Remember, Mum? How you used to do the laird's typing – that's how we lived, wasn't it? You did it for everybody in the village too, near enough – the school, the minister, Arnott's shop, the smiddy. And helped them with their accounts. You ran the place!'

You remember the typing all right. Good times! Battering away on the keys, the bell ringing at the end of every line, the carbon paper and inky ribbon, everything set up on the tea trolley with its extension flaps. Handwritten scraps of paper you could sometimes hardly read to the left of your machine, neatly typed sheets stacked on the right – like doing the ironing, you called it. You really enjoyed it, didn't you? Making order out of mess – and it certainly helped you quickly get to know everyone in the village. The farmers sometimes paying you in eggs, vegetables; Arnott's giving you groceries as well as a good discount; other folk giving you rabbits, fish out the Annan . . .

'Mum, who were the Callanders?'

'The *who*? Never heard of them.'

He's gone back to that photo of the man and woman on

their doorstep. 'Their names are on the back. I don't think you ever mentioned them and—'

'I don't know who they are, and I don't want to know.' You snatch the album from him, slam it shut and hand it back. If it's mostly people you don't know, you tell him, he might as well give the book to someone else.

But he won't stop. Next comes a photo of your cottage. Yes, that's where you live. It's yours. When the laird's estate got broken up in the eighties, Tom bought it for you so that you'd always be secure. That photo's worth keeping, you say.

'It's where you brought me up, eh, Mum?'

'Where *you* were brought up? What are you on about? Don't talk daft.'

But now he's started, there he goes talk talk talk talk talk.

Of course, today's really Monday. Monday. Monday. MONDAY.

Monday's always washday. Take the week's washing with you in the morning when you go up to the factor's office, then use the laundry tub at the back of the house in the afternoon. Pretending Tom was with you, helping. Pretending so hard that sometimes he really seemed to be there at your side, the two of you singing as you worked:

'Scrub a dub-dub, Three men in a tub . . . !'

'What's that, Mum?'

Dirty, crumpled clothes into the sink, the cold water turning your hands red-raw, the stone floor puddled from the wash being lifted between the deep sink and the tub.

'The butcher, the baker, the candlestick maker . . .'

'The – who, Mum? I'm talking about the cottage. See, that's me and my new bike on the drive up to the big house.'

Yes, Tom's helping you today, both hands at once, barrel-organ-ing the mangle with his little-boy strength, sending the squeezed-out water splashing down into the tub. A pair of small dungarees will be first to go between the rollers, sodden, then dripping ice-cold water as it's forced through. All the way in . . . and out the other side it comes, crushed and flattened into your waiting arms.

'. . . and there's the tree you were always telling me not to climb, and the laird's horse looking out its stable. *Rusty* he was called. Remember when they lifted me up onto Rusty's back so I could go for a . . . ?'

Tom celebrates by knocking on the side of the tub with his fist – *Boom! Boom! Boom!* Makes you both laugh. You take good hold of the dungarees by the shoulders and shake them, making them snap in the air, crack like a whip. Another *Boom! Boom! Boom!* Then you lay them down flat in the cane basket, the arms and legs dangling over the sides.

'Here's the vegetable patch, you wearing your big wellies and me helping you with . . .'

Then socks, underwear, pillowcases . . . till you've got the first basketful of the week's wash stacked and ready. Swinging it in time, off you go down to the gatehouse garden to peg everything out on the line. Winter days are fierce, the shirts and pillowcases freeze rigid in a few hours. Tuesday's always the ironing.

'She looked so neat and nimble-o

Darning with her thimble-o.

Dashing away with the smoothing iron . . .'

Last thing at night you set up the wooden clothes-horse in front of what's left of the fire and, just before you turn out the light, you wait to see the clothes steam in the heat as if they're actually breathing. New life – which is always a good finish to the day!

Most mornings, up to the big house and into the estate office to do the typing, the filing and accounts. Then the afternoons –

Tuesday – the ironing.

Wednesday – the cleaning . . . and typing for people in the village.

Thursday. Friday. Saturday. Village typing.

Sunday.

But not any more – since coming here the same week's become the same day, the same moment. There's no weather, no date on the calendar, no time on the clock. And the years you've lived through? They're here, and always have been.

Listen –

3

NORRIE PUSHED HER through the door of the bungalow and into a smell of new carpet, fresh paint and woodwork. There was a small bouquet of plastic flowers on the hall table. The living room was straight out of the Ideal Home Exhibition with modern-looking art hanging above the mantelpiece, wall lamps on either side, a beige three-piece suite, coffee-table with glossy magazines, white hearthrug, cream-coloured curtains.

'This yin's the real thing, it's fer showing people, the others are just bare walls and floorboards. Top tae bottom electric – ye want something, ye press a button. I tell ye, Maggie, yince the hydro-electric really gets going, it'll be free electricity and buttons for us all. See this?' He turned a switch set into the wall next to the kitchen doorway. 'Central heating. Ye put it tae ony temperature ye want. Let's get oorsels nice an toasty, eh! 75 degrees!' He grabbed her by the shoulders. 'Ye'll no be needing this onymair!'

Realising her coat was in danger of getting ripped, Maggie took it off and laid it on a chair next to the front door. Norrie threw his work jacket after it, but missed. Like an aggressive salesman showing how wonderful her brand-new life would be in this, her brand-new home, he then took her by the arm and hustled her through a tour of the rooms, stopping on the way to point out each labour-saving gadget, each clever new feature – the double-sink in the kitchen, the mixer tap, the waste disposal that ground up old food and garbage.

'See this hatch intae the dining room, Maggie? – was me cut it and fitted it. This breakfast bar? – me. This formica top? – me.'

In the living room he pointed out the side lighting, the fitted carpets and matching curtains, the skirting and double glazing. A large wooden cabinet stood next to the fireplace. It had to be the biggest wireless set Maggie had ever seen. Norrie switched it on. The dial lit up.

'Latest thing, this. Medium Wave, Long Wave, Short Wave – mair waves than the sea itsel.'

Once the valves had warmed up, he slewed through an electric storm of crackles and swoops until he came to –

. . . *and gentlemen. Direct from the heart of London we bring you Saturday Night on the Light – with Max Jaffa and his orchestra.*

'A bit of music, eh. Set the mood fer us.'

Steered her out and across the hall. 'The best is yet tae come.'

Pushed her into the room opposite. The bedroom.

'See this!' He clicked a switch set in the wall beside the door, and turned on the faraway bedlights. 'Magic, eh!' He grinned. 'And there's anither yin next to the bed fer turning them off. Luxury! Built the whole fucking place near enough, so I did. Me an Grace deserve it – no? Or are we no guid enough tae live here? Think we're no guid enough, Maggie?'

There was a large double bed with blankets and a shiny quilt, one corner already turned down in invitation to the prospective owner. Having walked her over to the window, he tugged at a cord with his free hand, 'Let's make us nice and cosy, eh?' The curtains glided shut.

'Fuckers that'll be moving in come Monday, that's what they'll think. That we're just working trash. Bairn on the way, and us still sharing wi Grace's parents in thon top floor slum. Running water in baith rooms, right enough – running doun the fucking walls.'

He pulled her over to the dressing table. 'Look at the pair o us!'

Wrenched her into position till they were facing the mirror, standing side by side. His reflection glared back at her, the bloodshot anger in his eyes:

'Working till we drop, and fer what? Fuck's sake, Maggie, let's hae yin five-star night in our lives. Yin fucking night, eh!'

From through in the living room came the sounds of the radio orchestra.

'Glenn Miller. We could hae a wee dance, you an me.'

Keeping firm hold of her he made as if to begin a waltz, then seemed to change his mind. 'Whaure's ma manners? First things, first. Get the lady a drink.'

With his free hand he drew a bottle from the side pocket of his jacket. He pulled the cork out with his teeth and spat it out. 'A wee toast tae us baith. Cheers.' Not taking his eyes off her, he took a deep swallow. 'Now you, ma lady.' He held the whisky up to her. She turned away.

'No tak a drink wi me? Am a no guid enough fer ye?'

'I don't want to drink, Norrie. I want to go home. If you let me leave now I won't say anything to Grace. Like this never—'

Next moment he'd pushed her down onto the bed.

The pub stink of him, the unspoken threat –

'Get off me, Norrie. Stop this. Stop it before you go too far. You've had one drink too many is all. Let's just leave now and go home. Grace'll be—'

'Like I said, Grace isnae here.' The menace in his voice: 'I'm no tellin, an I'm shair ye'll keep *stumm* if ye ken whit's guid fer ye. Right?'

Over his shoulder, she could see the open door leading out to the hall and the living room beyond. They were playing 'Moonlight Serenade'.

'A few drinks and a bit of fun – whit's yer problem, Maggie? Ye pan-loafie bitch! Easy seen whose side you're on.' The weight of him keeping her pinned down on the bed. He shoved the bottle at her:

'Ye'll hae tae get catched up wi me, dram fer dram.'

She tried to twist her head from side to side, but he forced the bottle against her mouth, upending it. Some whisky slopped over and ran down her chin.

'Dinna waste it.'

Clenching her jaw tighter shut.

His fingers wrenching her lips apart, and then her teeth – the tobacco taste nearly making her retch. Her mouth flooding with the harsh liquid till she almost choked. She had to swallow.

'That's the style! Come on, yin mair tae get yersel real loosened up, eh?' Tilting the bottle again.

She struggled under him, trying to push back, to kick out, but he held her tight.

Having to swallow again. And again. His fingers in her mouth, forcing it open each time. Another swallow.

'Come on, Maggie, guid stuff this. Better than mither's milk fer ye.'

His hand clamped so she couldn't spit out –

Tilting the bottle again.

His loud whisper, his hoarseness: 'Guid lass. We'll hae some fun nou, you and me.' Leaning across her, he put the bottle on the side table.

The rawness of his unshaven chin, his unwashed sweat-smell. His roaring whisky breath –

Pushing himself hard up against her –

'What the fuck!' The flat of his hand sliding down to press her stomach. 'What the fuck's this, Maggie? You're fucking in the club, aren't ye?'

She jerked away, pulled her knees tight up to her chest.

'Fuck's sake, Maggie. Fuck's sake. Up the stick, an yer making me work fer it? Ye fucking keelie!'

He was going to hit her. That was coming next. She could see it. She reached across and grabbed for the bottle to defend herself.

But he didn't. Instead he half-rolled away from her and started muttering over and over to himself, 'Fucking keelie . . . Fucking keelie . . . Fucking keelie . . .'

She wrenched herself out from under him and clambered off the bed. She stood up. Whisky-dizzy.

Meanwhile, the dance band music continued . . . it seemed to be playing right inside her now, inside her head, inside her whole body, like it was spinning her round. She stumbled away from the bed, the floor see-sawing under her feet. The whisky bottle still in her hand, she raised her arm as if that gesture could bring everything to a stop.

Next moment she watched the bottle shatter against the wall only inches from Norrie's head. An explosion of glass and whisky that spattered everywhere, followed by the slow *drip . . . drip . . . drip* onto the headboard.

His voice was a whine: 'Could've killed me, ye bitch! Fucken bitch ye! Fucking hoor! Fuck – Fuck —'

She heard herself scream back: 'I hope you burn in hell, the whole bloody lot of you!'

It was after midnight when she fumbled her key into Mrs McKenzie's door.

Having pulled off her coat and let it fall to the floor, she slumped onto her bed. She was shaking. *If she'd not fought back, Norrie would have –*

Next thing, she was sitting with her money drawer on her lap. The loose coins slid from side to side. Everything had started to blur.

Back and forth she rocked herself, trying to blink her eyes clear, but they blurred again almost immediately. Through her tears the silver and copper glittered, with here and there the red of a crumpled ten shilling note.

She was still crying when she heard the downstairs street door bang shut. Someone had come into the close. She listened hard. The footsteps stumbled up to the first landing. Then stopped.

Only to carry on a moment later. Was that *him*?

She wiped away the tears with the back of her hand. And the next time she saw Norrie? And Grace?

The footsteps had almost reached the top floor. Norrie, for certain . . .

Hardly breathing even, steadying the drawer on her knees. *Go away. Go away.*

'Maggie!'

The drunken fool was shouting through the letter box. He'd wake up the whole house, the whole stair.

'MAGGIE!'

She placed the drawer down beside her and lay flat on the bed. The instant she closed her eyes the room started to spin.

'MAGGIE, I'M SORRY FOR CAUSING YE BOTHER, I'M SORRY . . .'

'Miss Davies? There seems to be something of yours out on the landing – kindly get rid of it!' Mrs McKenzie was standing in her open doorway.

'SORRY, MAGGIE. SORRY. SORRY. SORRY . . .'

'That *is* Norrie Chalmers, isn't it? Frae next door?'

'Yes, Mrs McKenzie.' Maggie had to concentrate to speak normally, distinctly. All by themselves the words she wanted kept slithering across her tongue. 'Foll'ed me long the street so's I—'

'Get rid of him. Then get rid o yersel. A woman that's no married at your age – naethin but grief for us respectable folks.' She gave a sniff, then she settled for acid-polite English. 'Drinking, too, I notice. Well, not in my house.'

'B' Msss McKenz—'

'I'll take your key, if you please.'

Once Mrs McKenzie had gone, Maggie upended the contents of the drawer into her handbag. She stuffed her clothes into her suitcase.

Twenty minutes later, she was letting herself into the bakery – thank goodness Jean had insisted she keep a key 'just in case'. Without bothering to wash or undress, she stretched out on the chaise longue and pulled the blankets tightly around her.

You've made your bed . . .

There was no question of returning to Fusco's, she told Jean. Plenty unskilled jobs in offices – filing, reception, answering the phone, making tea. Or else she could waitress in a respectable teashop, a city-centre restaurant or hotel.

The first employment agency she tried was in George Street. Up to their first-floor office, then across the small carpeted hall to the desk marked RECEPTION. As the girl sitting there was on the phone, Maggie stood and waited. And stood. And waited. At one point the girl (was Miss Snooty Junior *really* old enough to have left school?) glanced in her direction, gave her a nod, then carried on with her conversation. Miss Snooty Junior had an impressive telephone voice. The call seemed to be something about last month's records, which hadn't arrived somewhere or else hadn't been sent. They were supposed to have been posted in good time. Mrs Somebody would have weighed them herself and Mrs Somebody else should have taken them to the Post Office at Waterloo Place. Three days ago. No four.

Maggie was about to leave when the call came to an end. She watched the receiver being set down in its cradle, the girl letting her hand linger on it for several seconds before glancing across.

'That was Head Office.' Miss Snooty Junior had a Reception voice, too.

Maggie was treated to a Reception smile and given an application form. Told to sit down.

Easy questions first:

NAME AND ADDRESS? She'd give Jean's bakery – just as well it wasn't a proper shop.

AGE?

SCHOOL?

Then came the hard ones:

QUALIFICATIONS?

PREVIOUS JOBS AND EXPERIENCE?

PREVIOUS POSITIONS OF RESPONSIBILITY / AUTHORITY?

POSITION SOUGHT?

From school onwards, Maggie's life was quickly reduced to a series of blanks. Snooty Junior glanced at her completed form, said thank you and repeated the smile. Someone would be in touch should anything suitable turn up.

Three more agencies, three more Snooty Juniors – same voice, same blouse, same lipstick, same smile. They all said they'd let her know.

Lunch was a Scotch egg, a half-pint of milk and an apple while sitting on a bench in Princes Street Gardens just along from the Scott Monument. She needed her gabardine buttoned up to the chin to keep warm in a sun that, at this time of the year, was starting to get past its best. From across the sloping grass of the gardens came the occasional hoots of trains entering and leaving Waverley. But it was restful sitting in the park watching the people, the pigeons . . . and she could have happily remained there all afternoon, doing nothing, saying nothing, as if part of an unfinished painting: *Edinburgh City Centre*. Then she'd *remember* – and, all at once, the picture seemed to dissolve around her, leaving her sitting on her bench, alone. She got to her feet, brushed the crumbs from her lap, then headed back into Princes Street and to more agencies.

Thanks to Jenners, Patrick Thompson's and Forsyth's, she managed to get through the afternoon. Whenever she couldn't face another Snooty Junior or filling in another form, she made straight for the nearest department store to wallow in scarves, perfumes, hats, gloves, shawls, working her way along the rails and counters until she felt better. Trailing a silk scarf between her fingers was like dipping them into the coolness of running water; when trying on a hat, she'd let the veil drop and was able to relax behind it, if only for a moment; as she dabbed perfume onto her wrist, she'd close her eyes, breathe in deeply, and let her weariness dissolve into Chanel.

It was getting towards five o'clock when she toiled up the too-many flights of narrow, badly lit stairs to present herself at Superior Employment. Her arrival was perfectly timed – no receptionist in sight. Had this particular Snooty Junior left early? Was she playing with her dolls? Sitting on the boss's knee? Maggie didn't wait to find out. Ignoring the brass bell with its notice asking visitors to ring for attention, she made her way along a short corridor until she came to a door which stood invitingly half open.

She walked straight in.

The name plate said: *Mr Wilson*, and this was Mr Wilson himself, she presumed, seated behind the desk, head bent over a pile of paperwork. Unlike her mother's hair-parting,

Mr Wilson's was ruler-straight and precise enough to look painted on. She had to resist the temptation to reach down and touch its jet-black glossiness to see if the paint was still wet. Without raising his head, Mr Wilson continued to scrutinise the form in front of him, ticking his way down the boxes of what was probably someone's job history.

'One moment, please.'

Each ponderous tick was accompanied by a 'humph' of approval whose seriousness reminded her of an elderly Recording Angel, one whose recommendation would be given great weight. Even though she couldn't read the form upside-down, it was clear that here was an applicant with no blanks in their life. Every box was so crammed that the handwritten details of their busy career had spilled over into the surrounding page.

The Recording Angel inscribed one final extra-large tick of approval before glancing up.

'Yes? Can I. Help you?'

'You are Mr Wilson?'

'Yes.' His tone was cautious as if he might have been about to add *but only on weekdays* or *only in this office*.

'My name is Miss Davies and I'm seeking employment.' She sat down. The wooden seat was hard and straight-backed, forcing her to lean forward as if she had difficulty catching what was being said.

She tried a smile. 'Your agency has come very highly recommended.'

'Experience?'

From somewhere out in the corridor came the *clatter-clatter* of a typewriter. The Recording Angel had his back to the window, which kept his face in shadow, reducing it to a mere suggestion of a face. His one-word question was expanded:

'What. Experience. Have you?'

He wore glasses. Small, rodent-like eyes – she felt their gaze gnawing at her, felt it scampering along the cut of her blouse and jacket, teasing the creases she'd ironed out on Jean's travelling-trunk-cum-table. His face remained immobile, his lips parting no wider than the minimum necessary to allow his prepared words their exit. Between words, the mouth stayed firmly closed.

'My experience?' She glanced beyond Mr Wilson's shoulder to the top storey and roof of the building opposite. 'I am a good worker. Reliable, honest and . . .'

'Yes. Naturally. All applicants are.'

'My mother always said I should be awarded an M.A. – Mother's Assistant – I was so good at helping her run the house.'

'And. Outside the. House?'

'Outside? Of course . . . I've been a waitress.'

The face arranged itself into what might have been intended as a smile of encouragement. 'Where?'

She said the first thing that came into her head. 'Lewis.'

'Lewis?' Mr Wilson's mouth seemed to savour the unexpectedness of this place-name.

'In the Outer Hebrides.'

'Yes. Miss Davies. I do know. Where Lewis is.' Of its own accord his right hand picked up a pen from the desk and held it in readiness. 'Silver Service?'

Doing her best to keep her thumbs out of the chips when serving the sit-in suppers was the closest she'd come to the niceties of Silver Service, but this was no time for hair-splitting. There was no need to burden her interviewer with unnecessary information.

'Yes, I'm experienced in Silver Service. And also acting as cashier, when required.' Well, why not? – she handled money every day, after all.

'Indeed. References?'

'Yes, naturally . . .'

She'd completely forgotten about references

'. . . They can be produced when asked for.' She and Jean could easily cobble something together, something that would include a glowing testament to her Silver Service skills.

'Hmm. Well. Now, Miss . . . Davies. A few details. Full name?'

It was Snooty Junior's perfume, mashed roses, which entered the room first, closely followed by the familiar blouse, lipstick and Reception smile. The whole effect was topped off by a bleached perm. 'Excuse me, Mr Wilson . . .'

'Margaret Davies, Miss. I have—'

'. . . Excuse me, I hadn't realised you were occupied, Mr Wilson. It's the Caledonian.'

'Thank you, Miss Webster.' The Recording Angel took the sheet of paper the receptionist was holding out to him. 'Seems you're in luck, Miss Davies. Perfect timing, in fact. The Caledonian Hotel is urgently looking for someone experienced in Silver Service and—'

Indicating Maggie with a nod of her head, Snooty Junior gave an emphatic cough, then leant down to whisper something into her boss's ear. Mr Wilson listened, then followed her gaze.

'Ah,' he nodded a moment later, and this time his 'humph' was one of disapproval.

Both Snooty Junior and the Recording Angel were now looking very closely at her, closely and in silence.

Mr Wilson was first to speak. 'Ah, yes. Indeed. Quite right. To bring it to. My attention. Thank you, Miss Webster.'

Snooty Junior inclined her head in acknowledgement, but said nothing. She remained standing at her boss's side.

'In these circumstances, *Miss* Davies, I'm afraid there is no position available for you.' His unexpected rush of words concluded: 'Nor need you put yourself to the trouble of returning here . . . afterwards. Good Day.'

Having pronounced sentence, the Recording Angel withdrew into even greater shadow than before.

Maggie was hardly aware of coming down the four flights and returning to the end-of-day bustle of Hanover Street. What had she been hoping for? Nearly seven months pregnant and unmarried, did she really expect someone to give her a job?

The downward slope of the pavement carried her on to Princes Street. Across the road stood the Royal Scottish Academy looking more than ever like a Greek temple that had been left for too long out in the Scottish rain. Over the years, layer upon layer of soot from the nearby trains and the city chimneys had drifted onto its pillars and walls, to turn into black mould. The grime was so ingrained that the stonework looked like it was being eaten away from the inside. The nearby Scott Monument looked just as dingy. If she herself stood in Princes Street long enough – and what other plans did she have? – would that black, tarry grit settle on her and turn *her* into a statue? A memorial to the Unmarried Mother, with her swollen belly for everyone to see?

She could imagine them gathered round her plinth – the Snooty Juniors, the Wilsons, the Norries, the Callanders, her parents and the rest of them – so many faces glaring up at her, despising her. The whole city and beyond come to show their contempt.

Well, to hell with them! Let them all burn, as Jean said. She wouldn't even lean down and spit on them to put out the flames.

PART TWO

Maggie gave up looking for work and spent the remaining weeks helping her sister-in-law as much as she was able, making the local deliveries, washing the baking bowls and pots, sweeping and mopping the floor every night, cleaning the oven at the weekends. The letters that came from Michael were the high points. They seemed to be from another time, another world – did they tell of a past she was in danger of forgetting or of a future that was still waiting for her? Last thing at night, lying on her chaise longue in the boxroom, she would read them over and over, trying to bring them into the present, trying to take their reassuring words and promises along with her into the night ahead.

With Jean's help she found a discreet nursing home off Minto Street in the Southside, and booked herself in to stay overnight when her time came. She planned to give birth there, away from the snubs and sneers of a public ward, and without the shame of an empty chair by her hospital bed when the proud husbands came to visit with flowers.

But then what?

The last of her Fusco savings would soon run out. Then what?

One thing was sure, cosy though the boxroom was, she couldn't live there for ever – not with a newborn baby.

The children's home was called Woodstock House. It was a

large Victorian townhouse that stood like a turreted galleon moored in a sea of green lawn while around it lay a scattered archipelago of hope – a neatly laid-out kitchen garden, a line of small brightly painted sheds along the back wall next to a greenhouse. This country mansion lookalike had been built as a trumpet blast of one man's infatuation with himself and his commercial rapacity, but with the captain of Scottish industry now long gone, so too were the finances necessary for the building's upkeep. According to Jean, the children's home was a private institution that only survived thanks to donations, mostly anonymous, and a dedicated staff. There might be a church involved in it somewhere, but she wasn't sure. Or else it might be some kind of charity place, like those houses for fallen women. Not that Maggie was one of those, her sister-in-law had quickly added.

The brass bell-pull slid stiffly back into the wall. The *clang-clang* and its echo tolled out emptily. Somewhere a child shouted, 'Ding-ding! Ding-ding!'

There was the sound of light, skipping footsteps. The front door opened.

'Hello!'

The girl was a teenager, if that – an upturned face that was mostly grin, keen eyes and a tangle of unbrushed blonde curls. She shifted from foot to foot to unheard dance music while shaking her head and clicking her fingers to keep time.

Maggie hesitated. 'Hello . . . I've come to see . . .'

'Yes? Plenty to see in here. Come in.' The young girl did a half-twirl and pointed towards a coarse mat. 'This here's for the rain. Mrs Saunders doesn't like rain, or mud. I'm going to be a chorus girl.'

Maggie wiped her feet.

The apprentice chorus girl high-kicked, birled herself quickly round, then faced-to again: 'Do you want to see her?'

'I phoned and—'

'Mrs Saunders sees people when people come. I'm just Donna.' She took a step back, then kicked out her right leg in a chorus-line of one. 'I'll take you.'

The vestibule had a tiled floor.

'Thank you, Donna.'

The girl carefully pulled the front door behind her. 'We keep it shut, for the heat.'

With a soft-shoe shuffle, the young dancer led the way into a large hall that smelled of cooking. Dim light came through a glass cupola above, the walls were a pale green and hung generously with dusty-looking portraits in heavy frames. Maggie could feel a chill coming up through the linoleum. The only furniture was a small but elaborately carved wooden chair that stood at the bottom of the staircase and looked like a make-believe throne waiting to be claimed by the pretend king of a make-believe little country. Parked next to it was a cumbersome, old-fashioned pram, dark green with large spoked wheels reaching high up its sides like a paddle-steamer.

The girl pointed to it. 'That's the Tractor.'

'It's big, right enough.'

Another flight of stairs disappeared into darkness below, presumably down to the basement.

Donna peered at her: 'Are you a mother?'

'I'm going to be – very soon.'

The young girl came to an abrupt stop in the middle of the hall, her arms arched above her head in a ballet pose. Her face turned in profile, she held the position for several seconds. 'It's not easy.'

Did she mean being a mother wasn't easy, or that this particular pose was a strain to hold? Could the girl be implying that she herself was a mother, this slip of a lass?

Maggie gazed round the uncarpeted space. 'I suppose not.'

The soft-shoe shuffle was then resumed until, with a sudden and unexpectedly grown-up sway of her hips, Donna halted outside a closed door marked PRIVATE. She curtseyed.

'In here.'

In one smooth unbroken action she knocked, turned the handle and pushed open the door. This done, she went tap-dancing off down the corridor, clicking her fingers in time.

'Enter.' A firm voice.

The room was slightly warmer, with a dark brown carpet and rust-red curtains that sagged like a pair of comfortably slack stockings. The woman sitting behind the desk glanced up – 'Be with you shortly' – then continued reading. A cigarette burned in the ashtray beside her.

Maggie was back at school once again, being made to wait in the headmistress's office where she'd been sent to get shouted at for not paying attention in class, or for coming in late, or for walking around in a daze. Though the actual details of the offence usually varied, in essence the charge was always the same – she was getting punished for being herself. This time, however, the punishment was for being herself *and* for getting herself pregnant. She stared down at the floor.

The superintendent laid the sheet of paper aside. 'Yes?'

'I'm Maggie Davies. I phoned.' The unspoken school-girl '*Miss*' slid to the floor where it was immediately absorbed into the carpet. Even the young sprite Donna had seemed older and more mature than she herself felt at this moment.

'Davies?' Mrs Saunders began leafing through one of the stacks of papers on her desk. 'Davies? Davies? Davies? . . .' She riffled through another stack. 'You phoned recently, you say?' Then started on stack number three. 'Ah yes, here you are. I remember now. You're due in a month and going to the nursing home in Queens Crescent. A good place, well worth the expense.'

Mrs Saunders' smile of approval at once cancelled out the schoolroom-strictness, replacing it with a feeling of warmth and unexpected kindness. Even the rain hitting the window seemed to ease off slightly.

'Thank you, Mrs Saunders. I wanted to do the best I could.'

'There's no current address given here. You're staying with your family, perhaps, or—?' Mrs Saunders looked closely at her. 'You do have somewhere to live, don't you?'

'Yes, I'm staying with a friend at the moment. I'll be starting a new job shortly, then getting my own place. Permanent. Somewhere near here, so that I can—'

'That's fine, Miss Davies, thank you. So long as I have an address for my records.'

Maggie nodded to show her willingness.

Mrs Saunders continued, 'You know the rules and conditions?'

'Rules? Oh yes, I knew there'd be rules.'

The superintendent took a puff at her cigarette, blew out the smoke and asked her to sit down.

While the rules and conditions were gone through, Maggie did her best to concentrate on what was being said and not let her mind drift to the ever-changing patterns the rain made as it streamed down the window. She wondered where Donna had sashayed herself off to . . . The cheerful yells she could hear, were they coming from a children's playroom somewhere nearby? Had the junior chorus girl actually been born here? She seemed almost like a ghost-child haunting the empty hall, the spirit of all the young lives who –

'. . . then sign here at the bottom,' Mrs Saunders was saying, 'where it's marked with a cross.'

Maggie took the sheet of paper that had been pushed across the desk to her. She glanced down the form:

MOTHER'S NAME —

MOTHER'S ADDRESS —

'Once the child is in our care, he will be well looked after. He will be *our* responsibility day and night. He will receive good food and all the comfort and concern one could wish for. He will be happy.'

MOTHER'S OCCUPATION —

FATHER'S NAME (*if known*) —

FATHER'S OCCUPATION (*if known*) —

'You can leave the name of the child blank for the moment. Just sign.'

CHILD'S NAME —

CHILD'S DATE OF BIRTH —

CHILD'S PLACE OF BIRTH —

'Once the child is in our care, as I say, you needn't give him a second thought – you can forget him. In fact, it's better that you do. In my experience, things always work out much better when mothers don't see the children at all. Only makes things harder. The more you visit, the more he'll become part of your life and you of his, and the more painful will be the final parting. Unbearably painful – for both of you.' Mrs Saunders allowed herself another deep drag of her cigarette and stared into the smoke wreathing between them.

'I have to stress, Miss Davies, that when it comes, the parting *will* be final. You will not be given the address of your child's new home, nor the name of his new parents. Over the years I've learned to encourage new parents to let the child believe that *they* are his true parents. It's kinder that way, kinder for everyone.' Another puff, as if taking a bow.

'What's this at the bottom about 'a limit of six calendar months?'

'That? A formality. Of course, the earlier he's adopted the easier he's adopted, if you understand me.' The superintendent smiled. 'Rest assured, the adoptive parents' love and affection for their new child will follow in good time. It always does.' A second smile. 'I can have him placed within days, then he'll be free to get on with his new life and you can get on with yours. Best for everyone.' Smile number three.

'But he won't be adopted just like that, will he? I'm not wanting him to be—'

'No, of course, not, Miss Davies. The child's best interests always come first. He's our prime concern *at all times*. But you can rest assured that all new parents are carefully vetted. We make sure they are respectable people, church-going and financially secure. Home-owners. Pillars of the community.' With every quality listed, the pointed look in the superintendent's eyes emphasised her real meaning: *We make sure they're everything the likes of you could never be.*

'And did I mention –' Mrs Saunders gave a slight cough

'– that the new parents frequently want to show their appreciation to the mother? You understand what I mean? Not that they will ever meet you, of course – that's naturally quite out of the question – but I will forward on to you any token of their appreciation. The amount can be quite considerable sometimes . . .'

Maggie had reached the cross marking where she was to sign. Her child would be well looked after, it seemed. For the first six months any adoption needed her approval, which she naturally wouldn't give. 'And after the six months?'

'Well, Miss Davies, let's cross that bridge when we come to it, shall we?' Having taken a final drag at her cigarette, the superintendent ground it out in the ashtray. 'Lots can happen before then, can't it?'

It certainly could – the moment she'd started her new job and found somewhere more suitable to stay, she'd be taking her baby back.

'All in good time, Miss Davies.'

Having filled in the form, Maggie signed her name.

When she looked up, Mrs Saunders was giving her a warm smile.

'Thank you, Miss Davies, and speaking on behalf of everyone here at Woodstock House, let me say how much we all look forward to welcoming your newborn child and to caring for him. We have the address in Queen's Crescent and will see to all the arrangements.' She stood up. 'It's been a pleasure to meet you, Miss Davies.'

'I'd like to see his room, please.'

'His room?' Pen in hand, Mrs Saunders was already reaching towards the stack of papers. 'Where his cot'll be, you mean? I'm afraid that's not possible right now. Disrupts routine.' There was no smile this time. 'All in due course, Miss Davies. All in due course.'

Maggie got back home to find Jean had a present for her.

'The answer tae yer prayers,' the older woman explained.

Sitting on Jean's baking table, the shiny black typewriter fairly bristled with keys, knobs and levers.

Maggie's obvious objection: 'But, Jean, I can't type.'

'There's a book comes wi it, tellin ye whit tae dae an see ye stairted. The book maks it look easy enough.'

'Books always do.'

'Well, seems it's maistly practice. When the time's richt, ye'll get yersel a job, a guid job. No as a skivvie waitress or stuck in a pub fou o gropin auld drunks. Folks in offices are aye needin typists – aa thae tycoon businessmen, bankers an lawyers, you name it.' Her sister-in-law gave her a gentle punch in the arm. 'Play yer cards richt, Maggie, an a smairt-lookin lass like you micht land hersel mair than just a job!'

SUNDAY

TIME TO BRACE yourself on the Rosehaven doorstep, press the bell. Stand on the yellow cross marked on the door-mat, show yourself to the CCTV angled above. Speak your name into the security grille: Tom Stewart.

Buzzed into the overheated hall, into the combined smells of floral air-freshener, yesterday's macaroni cheese, urine, today's stew and vegetables, laundry, disinfectant.

Not managing more than the first few steps along the cor-ridor leading to the dayroom before it hits you – you're about to throw up there and then.

Reaching the visitors' toilet just in time.

Forget about what your ex-wife said about your having no feelings. What does *she* know? Too many feelings, more like – and always too keen to share them. You just keep trying and hoping. And getting hurt. The lovely Janice . . . and now Mandy. A steady girl, a caring girl. Maybe that's what you need?

Feelings? Clearly you're deeply, deeply distressed about your mother's deteriorating condition. Visiting her at the cottage every Sunday without fail and now coming here to her care home is the hardest thing you've ever done . . .

Hours it seems like, leaning over the wash hand basin . . . one dry heave after another. Retching and retching. There's a slick of cold sweat on your cheeks. Your hands shake as they grip onto the porcelain rim. Your stomach's churning, but nothing comes. Never does. Hard work even to spit. You keep trying.

Then stop.

Because, quite abruptly, you're feeling fine again. Back in top form. A1 and then some. Yes, you've got the magic touch, all right!

Now, bin the paper towel – your face and your feelings at default setting once more, you're ready to go through and greet your mother. Bringing her a smile!

'Hello, Mum. How are you today?' You sit down in the empty seat next to hers. A few minutes' chat to get things started, and then you'll suggest she zimmer herself through to her room – no old biddies there, talking to themselves, crying and the rest of it. There you can almost pretend everything's normal. At least you've got her into a good place – costs megabucks, but hey, she's your mother. It was the best of the homes you checked out, the very best, and every time you sit with her in the dayroom you do what you can to shut out the worst of it – the little accident that's not been mopped up, the spilled food, the helplessness, the calls going neglected, the residents' feeding, bathing and bedtime arranged for the convenience of the staff. Most of all, the total dependency. The locked doors. The closed windows. The smell.

She's calling you Michael again today. Better to ignore it and tell her instead about your drive down from Edinburgh, the weather, the traffic, why you prefer the Moffat road via the Beef Tub to the multi-lane racetrack of the M74, show her your new iPad, tell her how you didn't manage to leave

Edinburgh till lunchtime as you'd had a late gig last night. Because she keeps nodding and smiling at the right bits, you hope she's following everything. Best to say nothing about getting the cottage ready for sale, of course, no sense in up-setting her. Instead, you describe a new trick you're working on and explain that nobody wants rabbits out of hats these days, not unless they're *virtual* rabbits, virtual hats and per-formed by a virtual magician! You're working on it, you joke. She doesn't always follow what you're saying, but you keep talking to keep things moving forward.

The drugs trolley's rattled up to her seat. It's Kylie on duty today, the small overweight woman, the one your mother calls Boss Beryl and who looks like a binbag that's not been fas-tened properly at the neck. Must be the Polish girl's day off. A real pity as she certainly brightens the place up.

'Time for your meds, Mrs Stewart.'

'I'm called Maggie, I keep telling you. Maggie, MAGGIE DAVIES.'

'OK, Mum, okay. Don't get upset. It's all right.'

Patches of red stand out on her cheeks. Clutching your arm so tightly you feel each separate bone in her fingers. 'Tell her. Tell Beryl there's no Mrs Stewart and there never was.'

While lifting a small plastic cup of water from the trolley, you give Kylie a smile that's half-apology and half-embarrass-ment.

'Here you are, Mum. Another green one, another sip, and you're done.'

Empty cup replaced, you thank the woman. She and her trolley move off to the next chair.

When you showed the Polish girl – Mariella? Marietta? – a

couple of simple tricks recently, making a pound coin appear out of her ear and then turning it into a shower of petals from her closed hand, she gave you a very big smile. Meaning that she liked how you'd touched her hair and her ear, and enjoyed the older-man confidence with which you'd opened out her cool fingers, one by one. She'd been impressed. She's mid-twenties at most. You could be her father? Her grandfather, more like! But so what? You can appreciate her, can't you? Those blonde curls gathered into a bunch at the back of her head, the loose strands framing her high cheekbones, that not-so-innocent glint in her blue eyes.

For several moments you and your mother sit in silence.

'Would you like some tea, Mum? I can ask them to—'

'It was cake. Jean baked a cake.'

That bloody cake again. If you've heard about it once, you've heard it a hundred times. 'Yes, Mum. Auntie Jean had a cake shop – in Haymarket you said, wasn't it?'

'This cake wasn't for sale.'

'No? Just for eating?'

'Eating? Jean wasn't going to eat it, me neither.'

The red floods back into her cheeks, warm-red this time. Genuine pleasure. And she's grinning: 'What a cake it was! Three layers. A sponge with cream and chocolate and marzipan, slathered all over with icing and dusted with hundreds-and-thousands. Irresistible.'

'Pity you never took a photo of it, eh, Mum! We could have put it into that album I—'

Her sudden anger. 'For the last time: I don't want to see any photos. I don't want to see any people. And I don't want to see *you*, whoever you are. Coming here, asking questions.

I don't want people coming, people not coming. I don't want questions . . .' The red in her cheeks has become like a burn mark. She struggles to raise herself out of her chair. 'I don't want . . .'

A moment later she has calmed down and is perfectly still once more. Completely composed.

'Nice of you to visit. What did you say your name was again?'

'Tell me about the cake again, Mum.'

'What cake?'

'The one you said that Auntie Jean made.'

'Jean made lots of cakes.'

'All chocolate and marzipan, you told me, and—'

'I don't want to talk about it.'

'Who was it for?'

'For Boss Beryl and the others, and Donna, too, of course. Who else?'

'You mean the people who're looking after you here? I don't understand, Mum. Auntie Jean died . . . years ago. How could she have known the people here?'

'Forget the cake. There was no cake. I must have dreamt it. All of it. I'm tired of your questions. I'm tired of you. Who do you think you are? Coming here and upsetting me – you're not Michael, you're not anyone. You make me feel like I've been doing the laundry all day, like you're squeezing and squeezing me to get the last of the—'

'But Mum—'

'Tom would have helped me. Sometimes I'd pretend he was standing there beside me on the three-legged stool, turning the handle while I fed the wet clothes through. We'd have had great fun together! The windows steamed up with the condensation so there was nothing outside, nothing in the whole world but the two of us . . . They'll be bringing tea soon. No cake today unless you brought some.'

'I had a lovely slice last time I was—'

'*You* had a slice? Not Jean's cake you didn't. She certainly wouldn't have given you a slice.'

'But, Mum—'

'She wasn't giving that cake to just *anybody*. And you – you're no one. Get out. GET OUT!'

Boss Beryl's abrupt tug-and-swish of the curtains.

'Been looking through the family snaps, have we?' She's picked up the photo album that's still sitting on the chest of drawers. 'Mind if I –?' Without waiting for a by-your-leave, she starts flicking through it.

You want to snatch it away. Whoever's pictures they are, they're not Boss Beryl's, that's for sure. You don't want that woman's hands all over them, nobody does. Her sweaty pawprints and snide remarks.

'Someone's secretary, were you, Maggie? Very smart-looking. Weren't you the heartbreaker!'

Only my own heart. Keeping its jagged shards clutched to you for most of your life, keeping them for the touch of Michael's fingertips to melt away the pain.

4

Aﬀter the early morning dash in the taxi across the wintry-dark city, across the Meadows and down a completely deserted Minto Street to Queen's Crescent with Jean's hand in hers to grip hold of at each contraction, there came five hours of pain and then exhaustion, followed by more pain and more exhaustion, and people telling her to *push-push-push*.

Afterwards, as she lay awash with sweat and still trying to catch her breath, she was told to look up for a moment. But only if she wanted to:

The tiniest mouth and nose, damp feather-light fair, hazy blue eyes. A boy.

Held up for only the briefest moment, held too far away for her to touch –

Hardly the chance to catch a glimpse of each other –

Then whisked away out of sight. Through to another room to get cleaned and swaddled up.

Woodstock House has been phoned, they said to her, *and someone's on their way.*

Maggie knew this was going to happen, didn't she? Her son going straight to the children's home? She herself must have arranged it, they reminded her. With Mrs Saunders at Woodstock House. She and Mrs Saunders would've discussed all the details between them.

Getting upset like this would only make things worse, they

told her. Always best to be separated as soon as possible. It was easier that way. Easier for everyone.

Of course he'd be well taken care of, they reassured her. Woodstock House had a good reputation. She needn't worry. She could be really proud of herself and it was time to let others take over now. She'd done all the hard work. He looked a bonnie wee baby and was going to be fine. Everything was going to be fine. She needed a proper rest now. Needed to get her strength back.

Maggie struggled to sit up in bed, begging and begging to be allowed to see him one more time, to hold him just once before –

All in good time, they said. *All in good time.*

Let's open these curtains a little wider so you can see out.

Let's straighten these covers and plump up these pillows. Let's get you comfortable.

A cup of tea? – with plenty of sugar, if you fancy it.

Getting upset like this wasn't helping anyone, least of all her, they said. Once she calmed down they'd leave her to have a good sleep. She'd feel better after that, they said. *A good sleep. A good sleep. A good sleep.* They could give her something if she wanted.

Totally worn out, Maggie fell back onto the freshly arranged pillows. She turned her face to the window, away from their firm hands, away from their repertoire of comforting words and kindness. Better to stare out at the November afternoon, better to follow the tracks of the raindrops streaming down the glass . . .

§

Her suitcase, a handful of painkillers, good luck and goodbye.

Jean had come to collect her and the taxi was waiting in the street.

Maggie stood looking down the flight of stone steps, the same six steps she'd toiled up the day before, more like six hundred now, and pitiless every one of them. There was a handrail, at least. She held onto it, quite unable to start her descent.

Taxi or not, she was in no rush.

A cold easterly pulled at her knotted headscarf and made the loose ends flap against her cheeks; she could see the clouds being hurried on, driven forward, scattered across the ragged winter sky. The wind tugged and tugged at a leafless silver birch that stood so close to a wall its thinnest branches scraped to rawness against the stone. On the rooftop directly above where she stood, gust after gust set the grannies whirling in their chimney pots. They screeched at her to get herself down the steps and out of their sight. Now she'd given birth she no longer belonged in this mountain refuge of soft pillows and round-the-clock care. *Down the stairs with you*, they shrieked. *Get back to where you came from.*

She caught hold of her loosening scarf. Jean took her arm.

'Yer gey peelie wallie lookin, Maggie. Shouldae stayed a bit langer, no?'

'At £9 a day?'

'Come on then, let's get ye back hame.' Her sister-in-law guided her to the top step. 'Taxi's my treat.'

'Jean, I—' She stared down into the everyday lowlands far below – the Edinburgh streets, tenements, her couch in the back room of the bakery, the job she'd need to find, the room she'd need to rent, the visits to see Tom at Woodstock House. Would he recognise her? Would he come to love her?

'Come on, Maggie, let's get you back home.'

'My suitcase?'

'I've got it. Ready? We'll take it easy. One step at a time.'

How shaky Maggie felt to be up and on her feet again. Her left hand clutching at empty air for better balance until she'd found the rail. Her right gripping Jean's arm, together they began their descent.

Two steps, three, four, five . . .

The driver stayed in his cab with his engine running for the heater. It was warm inside, thank goodness. Maggie slumped down in the corner. Jean stood the suitcase at her feet.

'Are you all right, Maggie?'

'Thanks, Jean. Taxi's a real kindness. A tram would have been beyond me.'

'A tram! Away wi ye!' Jean gave the address and they drove off.

'I was wanting to go and see Tom today, but —'

'Tom?'

'Hardly saw him for more than a few moments, but long enough to know he's called Tom. He knows it too, I could tell.'

'A guid name. There's nae Tom in the family as far as I ken. He'll be stairting aff wi a clean slate.'

Maggie leaned forward and turned to face her: 'I'll go and visit him first thing tomorrow.'

'We'll see. Ye'll want tae get some colour back into yer cheeks first, or he'll be thinking his mither's a ghost.'

A *ghost?* Maggie bit her lip, and sank back into her seat.

The door of Woodstock House was opened by the same tangle of blonde curls and smiles as before.

'Hello.' The girl looked Maggie full in the face. 'You're Miss Davies, aren't you?'

'That's right, Donna. Hello to you, too. Can I come in, please?'

'They never said, so I don't know. Well . . . (a theatrical sigh), I suppose you're here now. Mrs Saunders will have heard the bell anyway.' She stood aside to let Maggie enter. 'No need for the mat today, the wind's blown away all the wet.' She pushed the door closed behind them.

'How's your dancing coming on?'

'Blisters. Thank you for asking. Some advice – never try doing the can-can barefoot. Too many splinters.'

'Thank you. I'll remember.'

They crossed the hall. Though it was only a month since Maggie had been here, the linoleum seemed to have hardened to a sheet of permafrost and the varnished staircase become encrusted with ice. It was so cold she could see her breath.

'Heat's kept for the children's rooms. No one hangs about in the hall, so why heat it? That's what Mrs Saunders says. Sometimes I do my dancing here because it's a good big space – but only if I've warmed up in the kitchen first, Mrs Saunders says, or else my muscles'll break in the cold or maybe even my arms and legs. He's a lovely wee boy.'

'Yes. He's called Tom.'

'Tom?' They had reached Mrs Saunders' room. 'A nice name. If you want, I'll look out for him.'

'How do you mean?'

'But only if you want me to.'

Donna knocked and opened the door for her. 'Really suits the wee lad. *Tom*. Cheerio.' She shimmied off up the corridor.

'Cheerio, Donna,' Maggie called after her.

The superintendent was again seated behind her desk, her cigarette sending up a thin line of smoke from the ashtray at her elbow. She was clearly involved in very important work and made no effort to look up when her visitor approached. Her fountain pen continued to scratch line after line onto a sheet of headed foolscap.

Hands by her side Maggie stood in front of the desk, and waited.

Two further lines were completed.

She coughed. 'Good afternoon, Mrs Saunders.'

The superintendent didn't look up. 'One moment, please.'

Where the surface of the desk wasn't covered in papers, there were ink stains, cup ring marks. The right-hand edge was scarred by a line of cigarette burns.

Maggie was about to speak again, but stopped when the older woman put down her pen and reached for a sheet of blotting paper. Finally, the completed foolscap page was placed on top of a nearby pile. The superintendent laid her palms flat on the desk:

'Yes?'

'I've come to see my little boy. He was born yesterday, and—'

'Name?'

Maggie took a step forward, right to the front of the desk. She smiled. 'I'm going to call him—'

'*Your* name?'

'Me? Maggie Davies. I came a month ago to arrange for—'

'Miss Davies? I wasn't told you had an appointment today.'

'I'm sorry, I didn't realise I had to—'

'Perhaps you'd like to sit down, Miss Davies? You must still be tired.'

The chair she'd sat in on her previous visit was standing against the wall beside a large green metal filing cabinet. Maggie dragged it over to the desk.

Mrs Saunders took a moment to finish her cigarette, stubbing it out in the ashtray.

'Well, Miss Davies. How did it go?'

'How did –?'

'The birth, Miss Davies. The birth of your child. Everything went satisfactorily, I believe. Smooth delivery and no forceps – yes?'

'They said everything was fine.' Then she added, 'Afterwards I felt very—'

'The baby certainly looks healthy enough. No harelip, webbed toes or fingers, thank goodness.'

'I saw him for only a few seconds, he seemed . . . perfect. He looked lovely. I wanted to hold him, but they—'

'Yes, best all round. No sense in causing unnecessary distress. Can't begin too early to get the child used to being without his—'

'He's called Tom.'

'Pardon?'

'My son is called Tom.'

'Is he? I hadn't realised.'

'I want to see him.'

'I understand your concern, Miss Davies. Only natural, and many would consider it does you credit. But I must repeat what I said when you were here before, and urge you to do no such thing.'

'But he's my son and I—'

'I advised you to leave him with us, if you remember – leave him here and forget all about him.'

'But—'

'You do understand?"

Maggie said nothing.

'Once more, Miss Davies, I strongly urge you to turn around and walk straight out the door. Now. This very minute. Out the door and don't look back.'

'But Tom's all I have, and—'

'Like I said, it's time to begin your new life, and let your new-born child begin his.' The superintendent half-rose from her seat as if preparing to show Maggie out of the room. 'The sooner he can be put up for adoption, the sooner he can be—'

'I want to see Tom.'

Mrs Saunders sat down again. 'Adoption. This really is the best time. Everything can be arranged with the minimum of fuss and concluded in a matter of days. Like I say, best for everyone. Best for you and best for little . . . What did you say his name was?'

Maggie made no response.

'Best for your son.' The superintendent paused. 'Miss Davies?'

Maggie sat and said nothing.

'You're being extremely selfish, you know.'

Maggie gripped the sides of her chair. She sat up straight, met the older woman's gaze and held it. 'I'm his *mother*.' She could feel the beginnings of tears behind her eyes.

The superintendent leant forward. 'I agree, Miss Davies, that you're his . . . mother.' Paused for, but unspoken, the word *unmarried* hung in the air between them.

'Yes, Mrs Saunders, I *am* his mother . . .' Then, without waiting for the older woman's invitation, Maggie stood up. '. . . And, as I have already told you, my son is called *Tom*. I've come to see him. Now where is he?'

Mrs Saunders shook her head.

'Miss Davies, you must understand that I don't mean to be hard. I know it may seem like that. In my years here I've seen so many children . . . and so much unhappiness.'

'If you don't take me to see Tom this instant, I will leave and return with the police.'

The superintendent snorted: 'The police? You? An unmarried mother of no fixed abode? Do you really think they'd pay any heed to the likes of *you*?'

'I only want to see my wee boy. That's not a crime.'

'Your child is now my responsibility, Miss Davies – which means that *I* decide who sees him and who doesn't.'

'I'm not going to harm him. I love him, and—'

'Love him? You've hardly even *seen* him. You don't know anything about him. You wouldn't even recognise—'

Maggie jumped to her feet. 'I LOVE HIM! Can't you understand? He's my son, I'm all he's got.'

'Not any more.'

'Right, the police it is!' She started towards the door.

The superintendent stood up.

'We don't want any trouble, Miss Davies. We don't want the children upset, do we?' For a moment she seemed to have finished speaking, but then added, 'You mothers can only do what you must, I suppose.' She shook her head. 'If you get to see him this time, you must promise never to come back here again? Will you?'

Maggie didn't reply. She stood and she waited.

Finally Mrs Saunders gave a sigh, crossed to the door and opened it. 'Come on, then.'

A couple of small boys, aged about four and five, were down on their knees playing in the main hall with their Dinky cars, racing them up and down the floor and crashing them into the skirting. The smaller one had a harelip.

'It's a bit cold here, boys, why don't you go through to the playroom?'

'Yes, Mrs Saunders.' Dutifully, they got to their feet and trooped off.

'They're brothers, these two.' The superintendent began to go up the stairs. 'Refused to be split up. Each time Andy – he's the older one, the one *without* the . . . (she touched her top lip) – was taken by a family, he acted up so badly he was always sent back. No one ever offered to take Bobby, of course, let alone both of them together. A real shame. Little Bobby's a delightful child really. They both are.'

'And Donna?'

'Her mother died when she was nine. Father said he was a working man and couldn't cope. No relatives, it seemed. Brought her here to see if she'd like a day visit. Then never came back. Turned out to be a false name and address. No paperwork because we thought it was just for a few hours. Certainly never made that mistake again. This is Tom's room.'

A dozen or so mismatched cribs and cots were stood side

by side along the walls. The centre of the room was taken up by a table covered with several feeding bottles, a stack of clean nappies, a stack of clean towels. There was a desk light and what looked like a diary or some kind of record book was laid open next to a half-filled cup of tea. An armchair and small foot stool relaxed in one corner while a deep sink with draining board occupied another. The room felt overheated and probably neither of the two large windows had been opened today. The smell of soiled nappies, bedding and powdered milk caught in her throat.

A woman wearing a dark blue housecoat stood over by an open cupboard, checking through shelves of linen.

Each cot had a handwritten number affixed to its head rail.

Mrs Saunders called over to the attendant: 'Beryl. Queen's Crescent – came in yesterday afternoon?'

Aged anything between thirty and fifty, Boss Beryl was small and stocky, her dark hair set in stiff curls. Standing with one hand resting on her hip and staring flatly across the room, she reminded Maggie of a rather squat and angry-looking petrol pump. 'Queen's Crescent?' There was a swift jerk of her head in the direction of the far corner. 'Number 11, and he's sleeping.'

'Miss Davies won't wake him. She's just looking in for a *short* visit.' Then the superintendent left the room.

Without taking her eyes off this unwanted intrusion, the petrol pump lifted down a green blanket from one of the shelves and made as if to re-fold it.

Maggie picked her way across the room between discarded towels and pillow-cases heaped here and there on the floor, then skirted round the central table.

A baby started howling. Crib number 11?

No. It came from over by one of the windows, from some other cot, some other baby. She ignored it.

But then, as she hurried across to Tom's crib, she felt the unknown child's cry pierce her, *felt* it like a wound in the tip of her breast. Glancing down she saw a small damp patch on the front of her blouse.

Side-stepping a slew of wet-looking sheets, she almost knocked over a pail of water with soiled nappies dripping over the side.

'Watch where you're going!' shouted the petrol pump.

The pail stood next to an empty cot, the pillow almost small enough for a doll's bed. Crib number 10.

Tom's would be next.

Crib number 11: a halo of feather-light fair hair, scrunched-up face, wrinkled skin, patches of reddish pink, impossibly small hands . . .

She reached into the crib. More than her uncertainty and her awkwardness was her joy. Overwhelming, heart-swelling joy.

Nervously, her fingers brushed the warm smoothness of his cheek.

Boss Beryl? Mrs Saunders and her lecture about selfishness? – she didn't care about *them*, but was nervous suddenly, afraid almost. Afraid she was about to burst into tears. With Boss Beryl scrutinising her every movement, starting to cry would be the worst thing she could do. She daren't show any weakness, not here. If she picked Tom up too quickly, she'd be accused of trying to usurp Boss Beryl's authority. If she hesitated for too long, she'd be judged uncaring, confirming that she should be written off as an unfit mother. Which, being un-married, she already was in everyone's eyes.

She straightened Tom's bright patchwork blanket, stroked his uncovered arm.

Petrol pump Beryl took a step forward. One single step – and it was as if she'd been turned into a wild cat ready to attack.

But not even a dozen wild cats could have stopped Maggie now. In one smooth act of loving reclamation she reached down, lifted Tom out of his cot and took him into her arms.

'Tom, Tom,' she swayed him back and forth.

'Leave him where he is.' The wild cat was only inches away, hissing and spitting. 'You'll have him yelling the place down. Give him here.'

Maggie ignored her. Moments later she was holding Tom to her breast and, for as long as he remained there with his small mouth clutching onto her and sucking, nothing else in the world seemed to matter.

When he'd finished, she lifted him up close to the window so he could see the rain-streaked glass, the separate water-drops racing down the pane. 'Tom, Tom, hush-a-bye, Tom. Look!' she pointed to a clear drop that trembled, poised, holding itself together until it was ready to start its journey. 'Look – that's you!'

She brought him up close to her face to feel the warmth of his stubby little fingers against her cheeks and lips.

After watching the curtain of rain break into a swirl of colours where the glass was flawed – 'That's your very own rainbow, Tom!' – she whisked him past the petrol punp and out of the room, along the landing, down the stairs and across the empty hall, into the crowded playroom to show him to everyone, and to see the wind-up train set, the big toy-box, the stacks of wooden bricks. Then, his introduction into society complete, she brought him back upstairs again.

The instant his head touched the pillow, his tiny face scrunched up into a scream of such ferocity it hardly seemed possible to have come out of such a tiny mouth. His small body shook with tears. Howling, howling tears. Crib number 12 woke up, setting up a domino-effect of howls and shrieks.

Boss Beryl was furious. A feral hiss: 'See what you've done, see what you've done . . .'

Maggie had been pretty overwhelmed by the typewriter Jean had given her a month previously. It looked like a shrunk-down church organ, and was about as appealing. At first she'd ignored it. It might be the road to her salvation as Jean had said, it certainly looked unwelcoming enough. Like an accompanying bible, the instruction book was short on laughs and promised only duty and hard labour. Two days had passed before she'd finally put in a sheet of paper and turned the roller as directed in Chapter One: Getting Started. Then she'd taken the sheet out again. Smoothed it flat, re-inserted it straighter and tried a second time. She hit a key. Then a second key. A third. A fourth. She'd looked up at the paper: *mivc*. She'd tried again – *michaelmagie* took five attempts. *michaelmaggiejean* took nearly five hundred, it seemed like. That achieved, she'd started to work her away through the manual, exercise after exercise, till her fingers were sore.

'Got a tune oot o it yet?' Jean had asked as she left the

bakery with Maggie still battering away at the keys.

'Getting there.'

A few days later, she'd tried typewriting a letter to Michael. It took nearly the whole evening and used up a lot of paper. Her next had been handwritten. By the time she was ready to give birth, the road to salvation had brought her up to a hit-and-miss ten words a minute. Fewer and fewer mistakes, and each one swiftly erased.

With Tom safe and secure at Woodstock House for the time being, she now had to find a job – and as soon as possible

It was nine o'clock on the following Monday morning, the beginning of a new working week – and for Maggie, the beginning of her new working life. She hoped. She'd have to lie to them, of course, and not only about her typing skills. NO UNMARRIED MOTHERS WANTED was surely written in mile-high letters above the centre of Edinburgh.

After a last adjustment to her collar, she inspected herself in the mirror – the ivory silk blouse, black pleated skirt, patent leather shoes. Shiny black handbag.

From Jean: 'You're just the dab. Perfect.'

The mirror showed: respectable, trustworthy – a thirty-one-year-old woman who'd soon be turning thirty-two.

But a mother? – did she still *look* like an unmarried mother?

Drawing her comb through her hair one last time. Pursing her red lipsticked lips and allowing herself another glance in the glass. No motherly looks, please. Think single. Think confidence. Think ten words a minute. Think pay-packets.

'My seams straight?'

'Aa the wey up an aa the wey doun. Keep smiling Maggie,

like our army boys – chest oot and stomach in. Your coat, ma'am. And aye mind yer Rabbie Burns – *A man's a man for aa that!* A man's a meal ticket – plenty women marry fer it. Course, ye're welcome tae bide here as lang as ye want, Maggie, but—'

'Thanks, but come my first pay packet, I'll be moving into a place of my own. Then I'll take back Tom and—'

'—and then what? I'm telling you, yer only chance is to get yersel a man.'

'Jesus!'

'Or someone like him!'

Which made them both laugh.

Raw winter light streaked the length of Dalry Road, cutting round the outlines of the tenements' edges and corners, trimming the roofs and chimneys exactly to size. The pavements seemed to have been polished overnight and now had a sheen as smooth as the Union Canal. As Maggie turned down Dalry Road, she felt she was walking on water . . .

But she wouldn't be walking all the way into town on foot, not today. Not if she wanted to remain looking neat, crisp and employable.

The tram rumbled down to the foot of Dalry Road, went *clatter-clack, clatter-clack* over the intersecting tramlines at Haymarket, then trundled along the sunlit valley of Atholl Crescent before entering Shandwick Place and the West End. Past the Caledonian station and hotel with its uniformed doorman on the steps and the taxis lined up in front, and then into Princes Street.

The thirty-one-year-old, highly experienced typist got off at the bottom of Frederick Street and strolled over to the nearest plate-glass window. Against a background blur of office staff and shop assistants hurrying to reach their morning's work on time, she checked off her credentials one by one: the serious glance, the spontaneous smile, the tilt of her head. The poise, the confidence. Professional. Reliable. Dependable. Single. Childless.

By mid-afternoon Maggie had had it with slogging in and out of offices and agencies, up and down narrow staircases, she'd had it with Snooty Juniors, their Reception voices and their forms. Coming out of an office in Castle Street she walked down to Princes Street and was in time to see a tram marked *Morningside* coming along from Waverley. Good enough. Next thing, she was on board and soon turning up Lothian Road towards Tollcross, Bruntsfield and Carluke Avenue.

Ignoring the brass bell-pull, she let herself in through the unlocked front door of Woodstock House, slipped across the hall and went up the stairs without even a glance in the direction of the superintendent's office. Then along the top landing and into the dormitory, making straight for cot number 11. In one smooth sweeping gesture, she leant down and gathered Tom into her arms.

Mrs Saunders appeared in the doorway a few minutes later: 'You promised you wouldn't come back, Miss Davies.'

'I promised nothing.'

'She was here Saturday as well, and Sunday,' spoke up Beryl the snitch.

Maggie could once again feel the pain piercing her breasts and the warm wetness of milk leaking from her. With her free hand she unbuttoned her blouse.

The superintendent took a step towards her. 'Stop! I won't allow—'

Maggie held Tom in the crook of her arm, ready to suck.

'Are you going to rip my child out of my arms?'

The two women glared at each other while the wild cat looked on. Paying no attention to anyone else, Tom fastened onto Maggie's nipple and began to suckle.

'I'm warning you, Miss Davies.'

Without breaking eye-contact, Maggie shifted Tom's position to make him more comfortable.

The superintendent raised her voice: 'I said, I'm warning you, Miss Davies.'

'She was like this at the weekend, too, Mrs Saunders. Thinks she's Lady Muck, but she's nothing more than—'

'Get on with your work, Beryl. You see the trouble you cause, Miss Davies. Coming here, disturbing—'

'I'm disturbing no one.' Maggie bent down to kiss the top of Tom's head . . .

'You mothers are not expected to—'

. . . and stroke his feathery hair. 'How's my wee boy. How's my wee boy, how's Tom? Have you missed me?'

For several seconds Mrs Saunders looked on and said nothing. Finally she let her hands drop to her sides. 'We don't want any trouble, remember. Just make sure you don't get in the way.' She turned on her heel and walked out the door.

Maggie shifted Tom to her other breast.

By the end of the first week Maggie had a routine:

Up at 6.30 for two hours' typing, then the tram into town.

She'd get off at the Waverley end of Princes Street, walk up North Bridge to the *Scotsman* offices, to scan through the Situations Vacant columns as early as possible. Late morning, she'd return to get the first edition of the *Evening News*. Her days were an endless round of employment agencies, receptionists, application forms, waiting rooms, interviews. Queuing to use public phones, walking to offices in the New Town, taking trams to offices in Newington, in Leith, in Gorgie, Stockbridge. Come late afternoon she'd usually had enough rejections for the day and would take the next tram she saw going in the direction of Carluke Avenue, to be in time to give Tom his early evening feed. She'd wanted to breastfeed him, but after only a few days she'd had to ask to use one of the Woodstock House baby feeding bottles – her milk was already starting to dry up. She'd been given it, grudgingly.

Her nights were spent at the bakery table, answering advertisements in her own best handwriting, and doing more typing practice. Last thing, and when she had the energy, she'd add a few sentences to her current letter to Michael. Trams, telephone calls, letters, newspapers. Being unemployed was a full-time job. And exhausting. And expensive.

The closer it came to Christmas, the fewer were the employers looking to take on new staff. But Maggie kept trying. Kept phoning and being put on hold, kept being told the vacancy was already filled, being told they were looking for someone younger, or someone older. Or else they wanted a man. A bloody man – the answer to everyone's problems, according to Jean. Doggedly, rain or shine, she tramped around the city centre – George St, Hanover St, Frederick St, Castle St, the West End, the New Town . . . She went in and out of wood-panelled offices, some with fresh cut flowers in their reception rooms and views over Queen St Gardens; elsewhere she laboured up and down narrow and uncarpeted stairs, found herself shown into forlorn offices with grubby skylights, plasterboard partitions and audible plumbing.

Christmas brought a card and a small cake from Jean, and a card came from Michael – *My Xmas wish is that we were together* had been inscribed below the festive greetings in Lachlan's neat handwriting. She put his card next to the photograph he'd sent her in an earlier letter – a snap of himself as a soldier, standing next to an army lorry covered in mud except for where the sweep of its single wiper had kept the windscreen clear enough to see through. Beside him there was a road sign: BERLIN 867 Kms. The photograph always confused her, it wasn't the man she knew – his blindness, his dependence. Not even the handwriting on the card was his. Years ago, when the photograph was taken, she'd still have been living in her parents' house doing her best to get through the war. Re-reading Michael's letters, which she did, they often seemed written to another Maggie altogether, one who lived a completely different life. Briefly, as she read, she'd let herself become this other woman, allowing herself to feel loved and cherished and to believe that everything would end happily. This happy-ever-after Maggie didn't have to struggle through every day, there seemed to be no loneliness in her life, no exhaustion. Clearly she never wept.

For Hogmanay she was invited to Jean's home. At first she said no, thank you, she'd prefer to see the New Year in by herself. But Jean kept on insisting.

It was getting on for midnight when she left the bakery

to make her way to her sister-in-law's flat in the nearby colonies, just off Haymarket. After the bells rang out the New Year the small flat began filling up with neighbours come to first foot. Then the dancing began. An hour after she'd arrived her brother Billy still hadn't acknowledged her, let alone spoken to her. She'd caught him glancing over a couple of times, only to see him immediately turn away. Finally he came across:

'Well then?'

'Happy New Year to you, too,' said Maggie.

'I'm asking,' her brother continued, 'what do you think you're doing? Mother's heart-broken. Father'll not have your name mentioned in the house. A fair disgrace, he says.'

'So? I can't help how they—'

'You can marry the man, can't you? Tell us where he lives and we'll pay him a visit. Once you're married, nothing of this'll matter any more.'

'Like it never happened?'

'That's the ticket, and everyone'll be happy.'

'That'll be nice for them.'

She left shortly after.

Twice on her way home she was grabbed and given a New Year's kiss. Then, just as she was turning into her own side street, a group of first-footers called to her from the opposite pavement: 'Happy New Year! Happy New Year!'

'Happy New Year to you, too!' She called back to them, and meant it. Forget the past. Forget brother Billy and her parents, forget the Callanders and Mrs Stewart. She had the New Year to look forward to. She had Tom . . . and she had Michael.

SUNDAY

To make the best of seeing her, the best for both of you, you have to make the effort to block out the TV's over-cranked volume, block out the empty stare of the Murray twins, block out the whole depressing end-of-the-line feel of things, and cut straight to what concerns you – your mother. You can only manage a few hours every week so you want to make the most of it. No expense spared and coming as often as you can to spend time with her. The good days, and the not-so-good days . . .

Today she's been dressed in a pink jersey and M&S slacks. Best to catch her eye before crossing over to take the empty seat next to her. Try to catch it, at least.

'Hello, Mum!'

Nothing. Like she's morphed into Murray number three. Has she even noticed you've come into the room?

'Hello, Mum. How are you today?'

Still nothing.

Not a good day. Sit down next to her, touching her lightly on the arm. 'Really good to see you again, Mum.'

'When there's bubbles of soap, it needs another rinse. Another rinse and another good mangle.'

Definitely not a good day. Give her hand a squeeze, try to catch what she's saying so you'll both be on the same page, the two of you sharing a Sunday afternoon together in the nursing home. Making up for lost time, it feels like, all the caring and loving you want to give her before it's too –

'Can't abide that chemical smell of soap in clothes.'

'Remember that big block of green soap and the washboard, Mum? We'd sing, "Scrub-a-dub-dub, Three men in a tub" . . .'

No response.

Fine.

TV's even louder than usual, battering the dayroom and everyone in it. Better to take her through to her own room. Where's her zimmer?

'You're not leaving already, are you? Stay with me. They'll be bringing round a cup of tea any minute.'

'That's good.' Managing a hopeful-looking smile. 'Then we can—'

'I'll need to iron it. And a chicken. You're a man, you can do that, eh?'

'Do what, Mum? What do you want me to –?'

'One of the hens, of course. Kill it.'

A really bad day. A few seats along, the sexy Polish girl is trying to get one of the Murray twins to drink out of an orange plastic cup with a spout. A safety lid and Bart Simpson on the side.

'Need drink, Joan. Need meds.'

The Murray doesn't seem to notice her, the old woman's mouth remains closed and her hands have collapsed to a slackness on her lap.

'Drink, Joan. Help meds work. Drink. Drink.' The girl

takes the trembling hands and wraps them round Bart, raising the spout into position. 'Good, Joan, good. Drink.'

But the Murray's having none of it. Her gaze is fixed far in the distance like she's really somewhere else, like on another planet. Her eyes are wide, wide open – is it possible she doesn't even *see* the girl crouching down beside her? Doesn't even *feel* the plastic spout pressed against her own mouth?

'One med for finish. Drink. One med for finish, Joan, then I go.'

Probably the girl feels like ramming the spout full-force between the old woman's lips and yanking the Murray head back – and who could blame her? Whatever. She's a real stunner, and would make the perfect assistant. Even in these politically correct days a magician needs a pretty assistant to display the inside of the shiny magic box and show that it's empty, to let herself be lasered in half, or else to help you disappear in a puff of smoke.

It's far too hot in here, the sun's melted and is pouring out pure heat, the windows are sealed tight shut as always. What a place. Some of the Dorothys and Murrays are facing the TV screen and some aren't. Rosehaven social life.

Your mother's turned to stare at the TV.

'That letter's made her cry. The poor woman. Making her cry and cry.'

You look across at the screen. Not that again. It's a rerun of what had been on the first day you'd come to visit, the same US soap that had made your mother so upset you'd gone over and changed it to horse racing. Nobody said anything, or noticed even – but Kylie spoke to you afterwards, telling you to please not do it again. The residents might not say anything, she explained, but it would still upset them. If your mother gets upset again, she'd added, best to take her through to her own room.

'CAN'T SOMEONE DO SOMETHING? DOES NO ONE CARE?'

'We've seen this episode before, Mum, let's go to your room. It'll be quieter there and we can have a good chat together.' Taking her arm, ready to help her stand up. 'I'll make some tea, if you like. I brought us some hobnobs.'

Out of the corner of your eye you can see the woman's now finished reading her letter and is about to let it slip from her hand. This was the moment in the scene when you switched channels last time, but you can guess what's going to happen anyway – there'll likely have been some cheesy direction telling the actress to give the sheet of paper a very slight flick of the wrist as she lets it drop, that way it'll flip over a couple of times on the way down to the floor.

And sure enough, the camera follows its descent in slow-motion to show everyone that the woman's heart being turned over. Spelling out her grief / disappointment / regret / sense of loss. Whatever. A cheap trick. But effective.

No problem this time round – your mother's face has gone quite blank, as if she's been put into a trance. If only. Then you could keep her safe and suggest to her only the sort of things that'll make her happy. You want her so much to be happy.

Perfectly on cue, she gives you a smile. 'Hello! Are you here for the cake?'

'Cake?' You sit down again. 'Of course, I'd love some. Then we can go through to your room and—'

'Because if you are, you'll need a name tag. Security.'

'Security? I gave my name and walked in today same as usual. No problem, like every Sunday. I've been coming here for weeks now, Mum. Never seen a name tag. No one's wearing any.'

'Only the ones that need to. The staff, Mrs Saunders, Donna—'

'You've not got one.'

'Mine's getting changed. Seems there was some kind of mix-up. They were going to give me Mrs Stewart's till I put them right. It's getting made up now, it's all on their computer. MAGGIE DAVIES it'll say. Mrs Saunders is organising it.'

'That's nice of her.'

'Otherwise poor Mrs Stewart'll be walking about with no name – might as well not exist, eh?'

'Mmm, I suppose not. By the way, I meant to bring you some flowers same as usual, I'm really sorry. Bring you a bunch next time, picked from the cottage. Happy memories, eh. My childhood home, after all.'

'My cottage *your* childhood home? What on earth are you talking about? I don't know who you are, I don't know where you came from, I don't know anything about you. You just keep talking talking talking. More sense in what they're showing on the TV.'

Next moment she's turned back to the screen and probably won't even notice when you get up to say goodbye. Might as well take out your iPad.

5

J ANUARY CAME AND went. Then February, March . . .

She owed Jean money for food, for laundry, for tram fare, for the telephone, for everything. She needed new shoes.

Down to only one letter a week to Michael now, and not just because of the cost of the stamp. She didn't want his pity by return. Tramping the ice-hard, wind-hammered winter streets of Edinburgh day after day, looking for jobs that she'd no hope of getting, left her with no energy for evenings of writing bright, cheerful, hope-filled letters. Sometimes she felt like grabbing an office-warm, brittle-voiced, white-blouse-and-lipsticked Snooty Junior by the ankles and dangling the girl out the window to give her a taste of *her* day.

Tom had begun his stay in Woodstock House on the seventeenth of November, which meant the six months would be up on the seventeenth of May. After that she would probably lose him. She *had* to find a job. Then find a place to stay where they accepted children. She'd tell the landlord that her husband had died, or left her, or was stationed in Germany, or Malta, or somewhere far away. The details could be sorted out when the time came.

By the beginning of April Maggie was no nearer to finding a job, or somewhere to stay. Only about six weeks remained.

It was a bitter afternoon – no spring showers these, no gentle breeze. Feeling she couldn't manage another step, she made for the poshest agency on Queen Street, overlooking the private gardens. Not that she expected to suddenly hear about a job, but she knew the place had a carpeted waiting room with soft seats and usually a glowing coal fire. She needed a rest, even if only for a few minutes.

No one at Reception. Perfect.

She collapsed into the armchair nearest the fire, undid her coat and gradually began to thaw out. Quarter of an hour later she was leafing through a copy of *People's Friend* when she heard a quiet cough.

Snooty Junior had returned to her post.

Damn. Damn. Damn.

'Hello, Miss Davies. And how are you today?'

That *I've*-got-a-job brightness. Maggie glanced longingly over at the window. Then steeled herself to reply: 'Fine, thank you. I was just looking in for a moment to see if anything had . . .' Her usual query.

To her surprise, Snooty Junior smiled at her. 'Right time, right place.' By any chance, she added, did Miss Davies know *Blair & Blair*, the well-respected solicitors across in Abercrombie Place?

Maggie nodded vaguely.

Well then, continued Snooty Junior, she might just be in luck.

A moment later the girl had looked out Maggie's application form, then shown her through to her boss's office to be assessed for suitability.

Maggie's assessment took less than five minutes. Blair &

Blair, she was told, had been on the phone less than quarter of an hour previously. They'd been badly let down by someone who was supposed to start that morning and simply hadn't turned up. They were desperate. Miss Davies' typing speed? Her references? Availability?

Could she go straight round?

Blair Jnr looked in his early forties going on fourteen. His three-piece suit struggled to contain the overspill of a cheerful schoolboy chubbiness that was topped by freckled skin and ginger hair. No mistaking the public school sheen of self-confidence, however. Also, there was no mistaking the no-wedding ring – which Maggie certainly wouldn't be reporting back to Jean, or she'd never hear the end of it.

After all that time spent filling in forms and answering advertisements, she had her story word perfect. Her reference from Cavendish & Son (Realtors) in Vancouver, was excellent – Maggie, of course, had checked in the library to make sure that no such company existed.

'First-rate, Miss Davies,' Mr Blair remarked as he glanced through the painstakingly crafted catalogue of her professional attainments supported by a list of her outstanding personal qualities. 'I congratulate you.'

Was the cheerful schoolboy being sarcastic? She risked meeting his eye, and he smiled straight back at her. His public-school confidence seemed to shed its own glow upon the typewritten sheets, turning their inaccuracies into truths and their blatant deceptions into recovered innocence. Blessing them, almost.

Maggie went on to explain that, sadly, Cavendish &

Son had gone out of business when the Son turned sixty and decided to retire. It had been a small firm and her position as Mr Cavendish's PA had been most rewarding as well as prestigious. There had been no shortage of other job opportunities on offer, of course, but her parents were coming to that age when they needed . . . Well, she was sure Mr Blair understood what she meant?

The schoolboy solicitor certainly did. 'My own parents . . .' he began before trailing off to finish his sentence with a regretful shake of the head. He was now looking genuinely concerned.

So it had seemed best to return to Scotland, she continued. Having spent the first few weeks helping her mother and father settle into their new routine, she was ready and eager to return to work.

As rehearsed several times with Jean, Maggie now moved into full interview role.

'It's . . . life, I suppose.' She looked away to cover a show of awkwardness, a hint of momentary embarrassment. After a well-timed pause, she managed to gain control of herself, swallowed discreetly, and proceeded: 'They've done their best for me, so now it's my turn to do my best for them.' She and Jean had debated whether there should be a hint of tears at this point, and decided she'd best play it by ear. She dabbed her nose, struggling bravely to carry on: 'It's only right that Mum and Dad should keep their independence for as long as possible. We'll see how things work out – when I've secured employment, I plan to move into accommodation that's close by.'

Mr Blair nodded sympathetically. Maggie was then sent

through to the room next door to demonstrate her typing skills to Mrs Woodward, who was in charge of Blair & Blair's two-desk typing pool. While she showed off her by now reliable thirty words a minute, her prospective superior looked on, and smoked. A page and a half later, she was invited to hand over the sheets for Mrs Woodward's inspection.

'Hmmm . . .' A pencil mark, a large puff of the cigarette. 'Hmmm . . .' Several more pencil marks and several more large puffs. 'Hmmm . . .' A final pencil mark. The cigarette stubbed out.

Mrs Woodward laid the typed sheets on her desk. 'Mr Blair prefers a *one*-line gap between paragraphs, and so do I. But good enough, I suppose.'

Maggie was sent back to Mr Blair's office. The schoolboy beamed at her.

'Now, Miss Davies, as I told the agency, we are very pressed at present. Could you possibly start first thing tomorrow?'

For the first time in months she couldn't wait to get home and write to Michael.

It was a busy week. As well as working full-time, learning to cope with Mrs Woodward – whom she soon took to thinking of as 'Old Woodbine' – and visiting Tom in the evenings, Maggie had to check the Accommodation Vacant columns in the *Scotsman*, the *Evening News* and *Evening Dispatch*. She went to see five possible rooms – but either they were too small, too dirty, too inconvenient or too expensive. One landlord was too friendly. On Friday she phoned about a place near the Meadows, at the edge of Tollcross. It sounded ideal.

The rent was manageable and the location, midway on the direct tramline between Blair & Blair's and Woodstock House, would be perfect. The landlady was a Mrs McCann – could Mrs Stewart come round on Saturday?

Mrs Stewart. That was the name she gave. As she was planning to bring Tom to live with her as soon as possible, she *had* to be a *Mrs*. She was already called Miss Davies at work, but so long as she kept her stories straight, and separate, there would be no problem. And what about her husband, *Mr Stewart*? Well, she'd got till lunchtime next day to fit him in, somehow.

That night in her letter to Michael she told him about the possible room and asked him to keep his fingers crossed – for Mrs Stewart!

Late morning on Saturday, the final hour of her first week at Blair & Blair's was being ticked off one slow-motion minute at a time. Maggie watched the hand of the large office clock on the wall opposite strain to make the next tick. Then strain ever harder, and take even longer, to gather its strength for the one after . . .

Only 11.30. She *tap-tap-tapped* through to the end of another near-incomprehensible letter. Original went into the red folder marked AWAITING SIGNATURE, copy into the blue folder marked CARBON COPIES.

'You still live with your parents, I believe?' Mrs Woodward lit a cigarette and blew a lungful of smoke towards the yellow-stained ceiling. 'They must be . . .' – with her fingertip she tapped the dead ash into the metal ashtray next to her own typewriter – '. . . getting on in years?'

Clatter-clatter, clatter-clatter, clatter-clatter . . . Ding!

Maggie's notepad lay beside her, line after line bristling with constipated gobbets of legalise: 'heretofore', 'without prejudice', 'available to be relied upon' and 'our rights and pleas' and the like. It was soothing to let her fingers go *tap-tap-tap*, picking out unintelligible gibberish that required neither her interest nor her understanding.

'You're having to take care of them, I suppose.'

Maggie hammered out the next paragraph in one continuous burst:

Following our letter of the fifth inst., you are hereby called upon to advise by return . . .

'Can't be easy for you. A woman of your age, you naturally want a life of your own, a family perhaps and . . .'

. . . your failure to comply with this will be founded upon . . .

'I was spared all that, you might say. Father was killed at Ypres, Mother followed him a year later with the Spanish Flu.'

. . . without prejudice to any rights and any pleas and any costs and recovery of said moneys.

'I was nine.'

Maggie stopped typing. 'I'm very sorry to hear that, Mrs Woodward – so terribly young too.'

'Brought up by my granny. Ancient history. I was married at twenty and I've never looked back. Douglas came along at just the right time. When war broke out, he volunteered for the RAF and ended up a rear gunner. Came through the whole war without a scratch. He . . .' She paused.

Maggie leant forward, waiting for the older woman to continue.

'All those bombing raids, Jerry's Mescherschmitt fighters, barrage balloons, anti-arcraft fire – he survived the lot of them. Hamburg, Dresden, the Ruhr, Berlin and not even a scratch.' Mrs Woodward was no longer looking at her, but staring into space. 'Lucky, don't you think? Really lucky?'

'Yes, he certainly was. You both were.'

With unexpected viciousness, Mrs Woodward stubbed out her cigarette, grinding it into the ashtray. 'That's what we thought too, *at first*. I go to visit him out at Gogarburn every Saturday afternoon – not that he notices.'

'I'm so – so sorry.'

Mrs Woodward inserted a fresh sheet of foolscap into her machine and resumed work.

Maggie's typing was up to date – her morning's carbon copies in the blue CARBON COPIES folder and her morning's originals in the red AWAITING SIGNATURE folder. The appropriate envelopes were typed, stamped and stacked, all ready to be filled and sealed. Time had come to a complete standstill at eleven forty-seven. The clock hands just would not budge, and the final thirteen minutes seemed to have locked solid.

Her filing too was up to date, her typewriter fitted with a brand-new spool of ribbon in readiness for the brand-new week starting on Monday. Her stationery drawers – foolscap, octavo and quarto – all brimmed in readiness.

Tick —

'Your first week at Blair & Blair is drawing to its close, Miss Davies.'

'Yes, Mrs Woodward.'

'I am pleased to note that you perform your tasks adequately and . . .'

'Thank you, Mrs Woodward.'

The older woman looked directly at her. There was a pause as she drew on her cigarette, holding the smoke for several seconds before exhaling. '. . . and you know your place.'

Tick —

Without meaning to, Maggie glanced over at the clock in time to catch the minute hand jerk forward to eleven forty-nine.

'In a rush to go somewhere this afternoon, Miss Davies? Blair & Blair pays for your attendance up to midday today. Eleven full minutes still remain and it seems only fair that . . .'

In a rush? She certainly was. A number 10, 11, 15, 16 or 23 straight to Tollcross. She had to see Mrs McCann and her room. She had still to sort out the details of her *Mrs Stewart* story, and get them straight. Was there a Mr Stewart? If so, where was he? Same with baby Tom – if he existed, why wasn't he with her? She had to think and think hard. She didn't want to lose the room – it really did sound exactly what she was looking for.

Meanwhile, Tom would be waiting for her.

The weather looked fine and if she wrapped him up warm . . . He loved going out in that Victorian-looking pram that stood in the hall . . . She'd bought him a new rattle yesterday and—

'. . . if you don't mind my asking?' Old Woodward had clearly continued talking and was now waiting for her reply to something.

'Pardon?'

'Your parents. You were telling Mr Blair about them. How are they accustoming themselves to your new routine, if you don't mind my asking?'

Her parents? Another story.

'They're fine. It's working out very well. I'm usually home in time to prepare their evening meal . . .'

'They must be very proud.'

'Proud? I . . . I don't understand.'

'Of you, of course. Proud of their daughter. It's not everyone can secure a position with Blair & Blair.'

Tick—

Eleven fifty-three.

'Yes, I suppose they are.'

'Well, Miss Davies, I'll be going out to Gogarburn this afternoon, same as always. He's still my husband, after all – and wears the name tag round his neck to prove it. They give us tea and biscuits. I read the *Scotsman* aloud to him. News, letters page, fashion. It's all one to him.' She took a long draw of her cigarette. 'Then we just sit.

'When I get up to leave there's a kind of flicker in his eyes sometimes, like he knows I'm going away. I have to go, though. I have to. But let me tell you, Miss Davies, I occasionally wonder if he'd be better off without me visiting him at all – at least that way he'd not have the distress of me leaving him over and over every Saturday evening. Four years it's been now.'

Tick—

Tick—

Eleven fifty-five.

After one final puff, Old Woodbine stubbed out her

cigarette. 'Well, that's our weekends staring us in the face.' She almost smiled. 'I'm sure Mr Blair won't quibble over the last couple of minutes. We'll see you on Monday morning at your desk, Miss Davies. Nine o'clock sharp, remember. Goodbye.'

Coat, hat, handbag, and Maggie was already halfway out of the door.

'Goodbye, Mrs Woodward. See you on Monday.'

Rushing down to Princes Street, across to the Gardens side and wait for a tram.

Right – now to go over her story. Her *Mrs Stewart* story.

Her husband had died? Definitely. That was best and simplest. He'd died just before Christmas, leaving her all alone, a poor widow having to care for their wee baby. No calling him *Alfred* this time, and giving him a beard!

But what if everything worked out between her and Michael? She'd not be moving to Lewis so he might come to Edinburgh one day and –

A number 16. Take her straight to Tollcross.

It was packed, downstairs and up. Standing room only. Saturday shoppers, their shopping bags, their children. A dog. Two dogs.

How's she supposed to *think*?

Turning into Lothian Road already. She needs to think – but how can she get her story straight with all this noise and people shoving her, wanting past to get off, and the clippie asking if she's not got change—

One of the children's started crying, setting off one of the dogs. *Yell-yell, bark-bark—*

Which sets off the other one. Passing the Usher Hall. THINK! She needs to THINK! Mr Stewart should still be alive. He *has* to be alive. Right. But they can't be divorced. Definitely not. Would cause even more problems. And so . . . ? She's all on her own, and she's – she's what? But if her husband is still alive why aren't they—?

Going past the Tollcross clock already. She'll be arriving there any minute.

Then it came to her in a flash.

Thank you, Mrs Woodward!

She got off at the stop just past the King's Theatre, walked about twenty yards and turned first left into Glengyle Terrace. A posh-looking street facing Bruntsfield Links, with railings and steps up from the pavement to posh-looking front doors. Not only that, but it was a main door flat.

Mrs McCann was in her late twenties. Cheerful. Welcoming. The room she was shown more than lived up to Maggie's expectations and would be large enough for when she brought Tom home. There was even a wash hand basin and mirror – and she'd share the McCann's bathroom and separate toilet. It turned out that Mrs McCann had a small boy called Douglas. Three years old, he played with some wooden bricks at his mother's feet while the various details were discussed over a cup of tea.

Then came the questions. Friendly enough though. Concerned even.

Mrs Stewart's husband?

He'd come back from the war blinded, and badly wounded. Hospitalised at first, then discharged far too soon, like so many of them. Then, just before last Christmas, he'd had to be re-admitted to Gogarburn. The doctors had no idea how long he had to live. Sometimes he seemed to be on the road to recovery, but at other times . . .

Maggie let the sadness in her voice finish the sentence.

Mrs McCann said it must be so very hard for her.

Yes, it was. And . . . For a moment Maggie seemed unable to go on, then she forced herself:

. . . And they'd had a wee boy just the month before.

'Poor, poor you,' said the landlady, 'having to cope with everything all on your own.' She shook her head. She'd no time for these women who got themselves in the family way without a family, if Maggie understood what she meant. 'But poor, poor you,' she said again.

He's called Tom. He's lovely.

Mrs McCann supposed that Tom must be a real consolation. But where was the wee lad?

Staying with his granny for the time being.

The landlady looked puzzled.

Because, explained Maggie, things being as they were, she'd needed to take a job and couldn't look after Tom during the day.

Couldn't Mrs Stewart move in with her mother?

No, it wasn't possible. Because . . .

Maggie glanced out the window at Bruntsfield Links. To have the park so close would be perfect for when Tom came to live. Those grassy slopes, the walks, picnics in the shade of the trees . . .

Her mother? Think. Think. Why couldn't she move in with her mother?

Her mind had gone blank. Completely blank.

A car hooted out on the main street. She caught sight of a green Eastern Scottish bus labouring up the hill to Bruntsfield on its way out of town . . .

Because . . . ? Because? She couldn't move in with her mother *because* . . . ?

Then she had it. Because her mother lived out of the city, near Flotterstone . . . and it was too far for her to travel into work. So she went to see Tom there at weekends. Her husband – he was called Michael – she visited as often as she could during the week after work. Once she was settled, of course, she planned to bring Tom to live with her. Wherever she was. Would that be all right? She'd be able to find a minder in Tollcross surely? That way she'd be able to keep working. No idea when Michael would be able to join them. Her tone of voice hinting, sadly, that he might never come.

Mrs McCann said she was very sorry to hear of her troubles. War was a terrible thing. Then she went on. 'We'll give it a week or so to see how we get on, you and I. Maybe you can babysit Douglas one night, and if everything works out . . . ?'

They agreed that Maggie would move in the following afternoon, to be ready for the week ahead. As they stood up, she only just stopped herself in time from giving Mrs McCann a big, big hug.

When Mrs McCann's front door closed behind her, Maggie lingered for a couple of moments before going down to the street. Heaven stretched out before her. She had a job. She had a room. Tom would be welcome. From now on, life would be one long walk in the park.

Of course, she'd need to remember her story and keep it straight. On the tram to the children's home, she recapped:

during the week when she visited Tom at Woodstock House she'd say she was out at Gogarburn visiting her invalid husband; at the weekends she'd say she was going to Flotterstone to see Tom. A bit complicated, but couldn't be helped. Depending on how things developed between her and Michael, she would say her husband was completely cured, or that he'd died.

That night's letter to Michael would be signed *Mrs Stewart*!

It was after three when she rushed up the front steps of Woodstock House. Donna was waiting for her, pushing Tom up and down the hall in the Tractor.

'Afternoon, Miss Davies. Tom's all dressed and ready. I was putting in some pram practice for when I have a wee boy of my own. I told him you'd probably be taking him out. You are, aren't you?'

'Well, yes. I've been looking forward to —'

Donna parked the pram at the bottom of the staircase and rushed over to her. 'Mrs Saunder's camera's got one photo left and she said I could have it of me and Tom if you'd take it. Please. Please. Please.' She held out the Kodak Brownie. 'We'll do it outside and I'll just hold him. Maybe us standing next to the Tractor?'

Ten minutes later Maggie was manhandling the Victorian monstrosity down the steps and out through the garden gate into the street. At every bump Tom laughed and shook his new rattle.

'Sunny day – Holiday!' she shouted. The sunlight was cold, but bright, bright, BRIGHT. A clear, crisp early spring day.

'Left or right, Tom – which d'you fancy? Left'll take us to the shops and right to the canal.'

He shook his rattle loud enough to show approval of every possible option.

'Or we could go to the moon?'

For there, above them, no more than a faint and almost transparent smudge against the ice-blue sky, was the moon. He rattled again and added a gurgle.

'It's come out early – just for us, Tom. Doesn't show itself often, only on special days and only to special people. So let's give it a special name. A ghost moon, we'll call it. Come on, Tom, let's go to the ghost moon!'

The Tractor was a solid piece of engineering, all bulk and weight. She gave it an extra-hard shove and let go, 'WHEE . . . !' sending it and Tom trundling a few yards forward by themselves.

She caught up with them: 'Sunny Day . . . Holiday! Sunny Day . . . Holiday! We're going to the moon!'

Four brisk steps . . . and another firm shove. 'WHEE!' Like she was already pushing him on the swings, a swing that reached all the way up into the sky.

At every push Tom shook his rattle like a champion. The pavement was deserted. She pushed and pushed . . .

'When we – WHEE! – go round the next corner, we'll really start to soar – WHEE! – soar up into the sky. WHEE!' The Tractor was picking up speed now. 'Nearly there, Tom. Ready? Hold on tight . . . Here we go . . . !'

Turning into the next street, she could see the moon directly ahead of them, set high above the roof of a large townhouse. Against the clear-cut outline of bricks and chimneys it looked like an unfinished sketch, a hastily drawn scribble of light that might dissolve at any moment. Faster and faster towards it they went, her feet no longer touching the pavement.

'We're rising up now, Tom. Feel it?' Treading air now, she rose higher and higher. 'Don't worry. I've got good hold of you and won't let you go – ever.' The Tractor swayed from side to side like a ship riding high on invisible waves. The higher they went, the louder and clearer sounded his rattle. Maggie pointed over to Craiglockart Hill.

'Look down there, do you see the tiny trees, the dolls' houses, the Matchbox cars and trams?'

Rattle-rattle, rattle-rattle.

'Up here it's just you and me, Tom. No one to bother us, no one to tell us what we can and can't do. No one.'

The city was spread out below – a ruler-straight neatness of streets, avenues and crescents with dotted lines for houses, shops and shaded green for trees and parks. The moving dots were traffic. Down there were Mrs Saunders and old Woodbine, each puffing out little clouds of smoke at their tiny toy desks in their tiny toy offices and, a few inches over, just next to the splash of blue sea, was her parents' house . . . The Forth Road Bridge was a cat's cradle of red spanning a streak of silver paint spilled in the cold winter sun, and the Pentland Hills had been polished to a smoothness of moss-green.

'There'll be no Boss Beryl, Tom. No Mrs Saunders. No Old Woodbine. No lawyer gibberish, no rubbled houses. No bombed Leith, no Coventry, no London.

'The world's a ball that's got burst, Tom. We don't have to play with it any more. The ghost moon's so full of light it's almost see-through. Michael's waiting for us there – he's the man in the ghost moon. He's putting the kettle on for us, getting out ghost moon cakes and—'

'Maggie!'

Within a split-second they'd tumbled back to Earth.

A woman was calling to her from across the street. Coming over to greet her. 'Maggie, I thought it was you!'

Her mother's neighbour.

'Oh, hello, Mrs Melville.'

'What a surprise! Where've you been keeping yourself? I heard you'd gone away for good. London, was it? This you back up for a wee visit?'

Mrs Melville. Iron-grey hair brushed to a hard shell, face powder cracking around her mouth, her lipstick framing the unspoken accusation: *Your mother never said anything*.

She looked down at the pram. 'What a lovely wee . . . *boy*, is he?'

'Yes.'

She leaned closer. 'What's your name, wee man?'

'He's called Tom.'

'A lovely name. Hello, Tom!' She bent further down till she was almost under the pram hood. 'Come up to Scotland, have you? To see Granny Muriel and your grandpa?' She patted the top of his head. 'And how old are you, my wee lad?'

'He's just a few months.'

'Really?' Another pat. 'And is your daddy up visiting, too?'

'Just me and Tom.'

'That's nice. A bit of time on your own.' She gave Tom a final wave and straightened up again. 'I'll meet your daddy

another time. Oh, you're such a bonny wee boy!' She turned
to face Maggie. Her lipsticked concern: 'Everything all right,
is it?'

Suddenly Maggie could bear no more.

'I'm sorry, Mrs Melville, but I've really got to go. I'm visiting a friend in the next street. I'm late already. Goodbye.' She
took a step forward, pushing the Tractor. Then at once began
setting a smart pace.

Mrs Melville had to hurry to remain at her side. 'Here's a
thought. Are you free tomorrow afternoon, Maggie? . . . You
and your mother'd be welcome to . . . to drop round for a cup
of tea.' The older woman was soon gasping for breath, trying
to keep up. 'Nice Dundee cake . . . I've been saving . . . A
chance . . . a chance to hear all . . . your news and . . . if you've
a photo of your—'

Maggie was now a good dozen yards ahead. She called
back: 'Goodbye, Mrs Melville. I really need to keep going.'

'See you tomorrow, Maggie. I'll say to Muriel . . .' Maggie
didn't catch the rest.

'*Vroom-vroom*!' she twists the pram handle as if she's on a
motorcycle – a sudden burst of acceleration sends her roaring
full-throttle forward. '*Vroom-vroom-vroom*!' Tom's rattle
urging her faster and faster. *Rattle-rattle, rattle-rattle . . .*

He's gurgling and laughing fit to burst, his arms and his
rattle going like windmills.

Into third gear, into top.

Into overdrive.

Curve in the street coming up . . .

Leaning over to take the corner on two wheels, the houses
on either side blurring past . . .

Leaving Mrs Melville far, far behind.

Accelerating out into the straight.

Full-tilt round another corner, the two of them hurtling along faster and faster, rising again into the air, soaring weightlessly up and up into the afternoon sunlight . . .

Maggie raises her head to shout out loud: 'Ghost moon here we come!'

SUNDAY

ROSEHAVEN AGAIN. THE yellow cross, the bell. CCTV, the security grille.

Buzzed in.

Someone's singing to herself. That folksong about going to Skye. Bonnie Prince Charlie, wasn't it? Posh English words for something so Scottish. Elderly cracked-sounding voice, pleasant enough, but hardly *X Factor*.

Managing a good half-dozen steps down the corridor until . . .

Rushing into the toilet before you throw up. Hanging over the basin, dry-heaving, your forehead in a cold sweat, your hands trembling. Retching, and retching.

Like sea-sickness, but you're not sick. You never are. Hang in there.

Hang in there.

It'll pass. Like it always does. It will. Steady?

Steady. Better now?

Rinse out your mouth and you'll be fine. No matter how rough you're feeling, the adrenaline of performance gets you through every time. Three cheers for Doctor Showbiz!

A last wipe-down with the paper towel. Deep breath. Reality check in the mirror – colour flooding back into the cheeks, a cheerful smile, bright eyes. You want her to see a loving son, someone eager to visit and spend the afternoon with her. Someone who cares.

There's a genuine *Mr Magic* spring in your step as you stride along the corridor.

But your mother's not in the dayroom, not in her bedroom either. You find Kylie sorting out pills in the kitchen, planting them like seeds into their miniature plastic tubs.

'Can ye not hear her? Entertaining us all through lunch, she wis. Widnae go back efter, so we just let her be. She's fine, though. Gang through and see for yersel.'

The dining room's at the rear of the care home – easy-wash flooring, plastic chairs, formica tables, white Venetian blinds, pale green walls, the day's menu and fire regulations pinned to a green felt noticeboard. There are half-a-dozen yellow-topped tables, each with a posy of artificial flowers in a small vase. Your mother's table stands in the middle of the room like a desert island adrift on a sea of blue linoleum.

'Speed bonny boat like a bird on the wing . . .'

'Mum? Are you all right?'

'Carry the lad who's born to be king . . .'

She's far, far away in an elsewhere place that has no borders except for the table edge she's gripping as fiercely as if her life depended on it.

'Mum?'

Her knuckles have gone white. Under her blouse, her collar bone feels brittle-thin, mere skeleton.

'Over the sea to Skye.'

'I'll sit with you if you like.'

You take the seat directly opposite hers. There's no sign

she's noticed you've sat down, no sign she's noticed that any-one's sat down.

'What are you doing here, Mum? Lunch is over, the others have all gone back to the dayroom.'

'Speed bonnie boat . . .'

Has she been crying? If so, they were tears that have left no trace. But there's broken skin, a gouge mark as if she'd run her fingernails down her cheeks.

'Mum, it's me. Tom. I've come to see you.'

'Over the sea to Skye.'

'That's a good song, Mum, I don't remember you ever singing it when I was—'

'How the winds blow, how the storm roars . . .'

'Hello, Mum. I've come to—'

'Hardly a chance even to see him, only a few seconds because they're coming for him, because it's all been arranged with Mrs Saunders. What else can I do?'

'Don't cry, Mum. Everything's fine. I'm here to see you and—'

'What else can I do? The rain just came down and down at Silverknowes – I couldn't stop it. You can't stop the rain, can you?'

'Everything's fine now, Mum. Everything's going to be all right, everything's—'

'But I'll go and see him as soon as I can . . . They don't want me to, but—'

'Don't cry, Mum, everything's—'

'Mrs Saunders said he'll be well looked after. So don't worry.' She smiles and lets go of the table. 'I'll be visiting as often as I can, I told her.'

'No need.' You make a joke of it. 'Here's me visiting *you*!'

A joke? How many jokes could survive this room with its washed-out décor, its empty tables, Venetian blinds half-slatted to conceal the neighbouring brick wall?

'Let's go through to the dayroom, Mum, it'll be brighter there. Or your own room if you'd rather.' You get to your feet.

'My room's been cleared out. Nothing left.'

'No, Mum, no. No one's done anything, really it's —'

'My whole life like it's never been. How could they? My whole life, like I'd never been born.'

'Mum, it's all right. No one's done anything to your room. I've just been there and it's the same as always. Let's go through and you can see for yourself. We'll get you settled.'

She'll need your hand under her arm to help her stand up. There's a puddle of spilt soup and flecks of scattered rice where she's been sitting.

Putting your arm round her and taking gentle hold of her elbow to give support, it feels like you're cradling the fragility of a bird's egg in your hand. One slow step at a time, you begin the laborious journey to the door, guiding her between the tables set with unattended cutlery, with flowers that never need watering. So near-weightless she seems, that you feel she might rise up into the air at her next step and float away out of reach . . .

She stumbles into one of the plastic chairs –

'Take your time, Mum. No rush.'

'No need to squeeze the life out of me,' she snaps. 'I can manage quite well, thank you. I'm going home, amn't I?' She's watching everything now, nervous and alert, treading with caution around another chair while clutching your arm.

'We can stop whenever you want. There's no rush, Mum. We've all afternoon.'

'All afternoon? Have we?'

'Yes, of course. I'll be with you for hours yet, all afternoon like I say. And we can make it longer if you want and . . .'

Not too long, though. You're seeing the lovely Mandy at Whigham's for drinks, then off to that new Italian along Shandwick Place.

She's come to a halt in the doorway, hesitating, not wanting to leave the dining room.

'That's it, Mum. Just like you taught me – *Look left, look right, then left again.* We'll get there.'

Safely out into the hall. To your right's the dayroom with the door standing wide open as usual and the TV unloading its noise over the elderly women propped up in their chairs, lining the walls. Not another afternoon in there. You couldn't bear it. You steer her to the left in the direction of her room.

'Someone's expecting us?'

'What's that, Mum? Who'd be expecting us? We'll be sitting together, just the two of us. I'll make us some tea. I've brought biscuits, chocolate digestives.' Keeping you both moving down the corridor.

'Will they let us in?'

'Who?'

She's stopped. Won't move a step. 'They know I'm coming. They've been told all about me. They'll be waiting. Suppose they slam the door in my face again? Suppose they—'

'Your bedroom door? No one'll do that, don't worry. Anyway, I'm here and I'll sort out anyone who tries to—'

'The handrail's here for when it starts to get rough, which it can do sometimes. I'll keep good hold, just in case.'

'Come on, Mum, we can't just stop here in the middle of nowhere.'

'So cold here.' She's started shivering. 'But at least I brought my coat and scarf. Why won't the sun come out? What if they don't let us in? We're so far from Edinburgh and—'

'Listen, Mum. We're going to your room, that's all. No one else'll be there. Be just the two of us, believe me.'

'No one else? You mean there'll be no one to let us in?' Her lips begin to tremble.

'There'll be me, Mum. And you. We'll sit together and talk like usual. We'll have tea and chocolate digestives.'

'But if no one's there how'll we get in?'

'We're there already. See, the door's standing open for us. No problem.' You manage to help her in.

Still clutching your arm for support, she works her way round the furniture in her room, running her fingers across the top of the chest of drawers, opening and closing the wardrobe door, reaching up to straighten a picture, a seascape that's mostly clouds, touching the playing cards on her tea-trolley. Finally she sits down in her chair. 'This *is* my room, isn't it! I'm so glad to be back here. Everything's going to be all right now. I know it.' The smile she gives you lights up her face.

The photo album's opened at that couple standing in front of their house. She couldn't remember anything last time, but maybe you'll have more luck today? They look friendly enough. Definitely not in the city, you point out. You slide it out of its plastic sleeve so she can have a closer look. The man and woman are both well into their fifties.

'So, Mum. The mysterious Callanders – who are they? Really bleak-looking place, not a tree in sight, a bit like Orkney maybe or Lewis—'

'Shut up! Shut up! You go on and on and on about them. I've never met them, don't want to meet them.' She pauses. 'I know what, let's get rid of them once and for all . . .' And before you can stop her, she's grabbed the photo and ripped it in half. Then in half again. Her hands and arms shaking, her cheeks flushed red. 'Burn them. Burn the pair of them, then maybe you'll shut up about them.'

Some of the pieces have fallen on her lap, others on the floor at her feet. You're reaching down to gather them –

'Leave them. They're nothing, they never were,' she hisses. 'Nothing. Nothing. Nothing.' She starts ripping them into even smaller pieces.

'It's all right, Mum. We can leave the photos.' You take her hands in yours to steady them. 'We can just sit and—'

She snatches her hand free. 'Go on, make yourself useful.' Spittle flies from her mouth: 'Get us some matches!'

When you return a few minutes later with Kylie, you find your mother sitting straight up in her seat, a smile on her face.

'Hello, Beryl.'

There's no sign of the torn up photograph, or the red album.

'Whit've we been up tae, Maggie? Yer son said something aboot yer gettin upset an wantin matches? Ye ken we dinna allow—'

'Matches? I'm quite warm enough, thank you, Beryl. We've central heating here – don't need fires. All that mess with soot and smoke and the grate needing cleaned out every morning.' She looks at the two of you in turn. 'I'm fine. Never felt better.'

And it's true. You can see that she looks utterly content. A moment later she's taken your hands in hers and lifted them to her face. She draws them slowly across her eyelids, her cheeks, her lips . . .

'It's so very good to see you again, Michael.'

Your father again. She keeps thinking that you –

'Stay here with me, Michael. Please.'

'Yes, I will.' What else can you say?

6

MAGGIE TYPED AND filed her way through the next week. She visited Tom. She wrote Michael several letters, double-sided sheets crammed with all sorts of hopes and possibilities, with her love for him, her longing for the three of them to be a family. It *would* happen. Their longed-for life together lay only just beyond this one same day that kept repeating itself over and over – a day of working, shopping, visiting Woodstock House, cooking her evening meal on the twin-ring electric Belling, keeping her bedsit clean. Soon, soon.

Spring was in the air and she walked to work enjoying the morning sunshine and freshness, and to save money. She'd do her best to start to paying Jean back and also try to put at least ten shillings into a Post Office account every week. Best of all, Tom's six months at Woodstock House had another whole month to run – so she would be able to remove him in good time!

She babysat Douglas on the Wednesday evening. It went well. Mrs McCann was pleased. 'You must call me Sheila.'

Afterwards, her landlady made the most unexpected and wonderful suggestion.

To be sure of catching Mrs Saunders in good time the following day, Maggie pretended she had an urgent dentist's appointment, and was already on a tram to Woodstock House by mid-afternoon.

The moment she'd taken her usual seat at the front she pictured Tom, fast asleep in cot number 11. How would he be today? He seemed to have changed a little each time she saw him, grown a little more, learned new gurgles and grins, new ways of grasping her fingers. When she left him, it felt like he was being wrenched afresh out of her body. Re-opening a birth wound that never had a chance to heal.

But not any more.

She imagined herself lifting him into her arms – and as she did so, the tram and the busy street outside dissolved around her until there were no other passengers, no windows, no solid steel floor, no metal rails beneath nor any sparking electrics overhead. Nothing mattered but the moment when Tom would open his eyes and see her – and, with every passing second, that moment was coming nearer and nearer. Soon it was no longer the tram that was swaying from side to side, but Maggie herself rocking him in her arms. Nothing else existed as she whispered his name over and over under her breath. This was going to be the best weekend ever.

She rushed into the children's home and straight to the superintendent's office. It turned out that Mrs Saunders was busy at present, but would see her in half an hour.

Having taken Tom for a short walk along the canal in the Tractor, Maggie returned him to his dormitory, settled him in his cot and went downstairs. For once, the superintendent was bound to be pleased with her – the six months would soon be up and here she was, preparing to take Tom back.

'Really, Miss Davies?' Mrs Saunders took a cigarette from the packet on her desk, lit it and blew out the smoke in a slow, steady stream. For a moment they both watched it curl in the air between them. 'For the weekend, you say? Your landlady suggested it? A "try-out", like something you might get on approval from Jenners or PT's, is that what you mean?'

'No, of course not. It's to see how he gets on so that the next time—'

'The *next* time?' Another lengthy drag on her cigarette. 'Do you seriously think you can just waltz in here, tell me some story about your landlady and expect to be allowed to waltz straight back out the door, carrying Tom?'

'No, it's not like—'

'It certainly isn't. There are procedures.' Mrs Saunders looked her full in the face: 'And then, of course, there's *you*.'

'Me? But what have I . . .?'

'Well, Miss Davies, how can I put this without seeming to cause offence?' The superintendent paused. 'Whatever happens, or does *not* happen, will depend on whether we decide if you're a fit mother or not.'

'But I love him.'

'Love? That's the easy bit. Love's never enough and usually ends up causing more problems than it solves. In Tom's case we're well past the maternal love stage. Different when he was a newborn baby; then you were free to choose to look after him – and if you remember, you chose not to.'

'But that's not what—'

'We've cared for Tom, looked after him day and night. In normal circumstances he would've been adopted long ago,

Miss Davies. But we've been very patient with you, letting you come and go as you please, letting you take him for a quick tour round the block . . .' she paused. 'And now your landlady's feeling in a good mood, here you are, telling me you fancy having him home for the weekend.'

'But I'm his mother and—'

Mrs Saunders held up her hand for silence.

'That, Miss Davies, remains to be seen. I grant that whenever you honour us with your presence he's very pleased to see you . . .'

'Yes, he is, always, and—'

Again the hand was held up. 'That's only natural. But you know nothing of what goes on after you leave – how he cries and screams and won't let anyone hold him. Throws his toys at the other children, takes theirs and pulls them apart, bangs his head against the wall and—'

'No. Tom's not like that. He—'

'Don't you understand? Each time he sees you leaving, he really believes he'll never see you again. Never. You've abandoned him not once, but a hundred times.'

'I've not abandoned him. I come as often as I can. It took ages to find a job, but now that I've managed to—'

'You show up – and he's ecstatic. Naturally. It's like you've risen from the dead.' The older woman leant closer. 'Let me tell you, Miss Davies, an infant can take only so much ecstasy and grief, only so much loss. God only knows what he'll be like when he grows up.'

'But that's why I'm wanting to—'

'And the man?'

'What man?'

'Tom's father, naturally. Assuming, that is, you know who—'

'How dare you! Of course I know who his father is!'

'Had himself a very late war, did he? Only got demobbed a few days ago?'

Maggie gritted her teeth. The woman was simply goading her.

'Saving up for the tram fare to visit his son, is he?'

Maggie gripped the edge of the chair to stop herself answering back. Whatever she said would be wrong.

With exaggerated calm Mrs Saunders turned to glance out of the window before continuing, 'I'm going on holiday soon. My husband and I are spending a long weekend with friends. Do you know Skye, Miss Davies?'

Sky? What had the sky to do with anything? For a moment Maggie pictured the superintendent and her friends drifting at their ease, perfectly at home among the clouds. That was Mrs Saunders' charmed life – holidays, friends, permanent sunshine.

'No, I don't.'

'Lovely place. But even if it wasn't, even if it was a total hell-hole – pardon my French – I know I'd still be having myself a ball. Why? Because I won't be here. I won't be having to deal with the likes of you.'

At once Maggie was half out of her seat, both hands on the superintendent's desk. 'What do you mean, *the likes of*—?'

Seeming not to notice the effect of her words, Mrs Saunders continued: 'The couple who adopt Tom – and I may as well tell you that there are several couples extremely keen to . . .'

Maggie sat back down again. *Several couples?*

'. . . will be a *real* couple. Married, settled, respectable. Able to give Tom a good home, eager to support our work here . . .'

Several couples . . . a good home?

'. . . and doubtless keen to express their gratitude to you.'

Maggie glared at the superintendent. 'Yes, you told me all this the first time.'

'Come in very handy for a smart new outfit and some high heels for the evening.'

'You think I'd sell my son for a new pair of shoes!'

'Not interested? Well, suit yourself. As a charitable institution we can't afford to be so sniffy. *We* need all the help we can get.' Mrs Saunders picked up her pen and resumed her paperwork.

'Still here?' She laid the pen down again a moment later. 'Well, Miss Davies, perhaps you'd care to explain why you and your gentleman friend *aren't* getting married?'

Maggie had run out of words.

'No? Then let me guess . . .' The superintendent took a deep drag of her cigarette and blew out the smoke in a steady jet, then stubbed it out. 'He's already married, isn't he?'

Mrs Saunders waited for her reply, hand poised in mid-air as if ready to remove Maggie from Tom's life for ever with a single stroke of a pen.

Maggie felt a wave of total exhaustion pass over her. 'The man's dead.' She stood up. 'Enjoy Skye.'

She left.

The following day, Maggie had to stay after work to make up for leaving early the day before, and so she arrived at Woodstock House much later than usual. For the first time, she found the front door locked.

But it couldn't be.

She tried the handle again.

Firmly locked.

She reached for the bell pull.

Its dull *jangle-jangle* tolled in the empty hall, to be answered almost at once by a scamper of footsteps coming to the door. Donna's welcoming smile was accompanied by a most elaborate curtsey.

'Hello, Miss Davies. I'm practising for my first ball.'

'Very good, Donna. I'm sure you'll have all the young men at your feet.' Maggie moved to go in.

The young chorus girl-cum-debutante didn't stand aside to let her pass. 'I'm sorry, but Mrs Saunders said that if you came, you were please to wait.'

Before Maggie realised what was happening, the door was closed again.

What was she to wait for? She was here to see Tom, same as usual. Nothing was different. She'd come to take him for an evening walk like she'd done dozens of times before.

One good strong tug at the bell-pull would set it jangling like a demented Big Ben. No keeping her waiting after that!

She took hold of the bell-pull and was about to –

When she stopped herself.

Too much noise and she'd probably wake the younger children. And as for Mrs Saunders . . . After their conversation yesterday, who knew what the old battle-axe might do if she got annoyed – maybe not let her see Tom at all?

But supposing he was ill? Mumps, chickenpox, measles . . .

The door opened again.

'If you came they said to tell you that Tom has a bit of a cold today, but he'll be fine. Nothing to worry about, and this is for you.' Donna held out a sealed white envelope: MISS MARGARET DAVIES.

Maggie ripped it open. Headed notepaper, stiff. Typed.

Dear Miss Davies . . . over six calendar months since . . . the contract dated 15th October 1949.

She had to start reading it again: *Dear Miss Davies* – two short paragraphs, and signed *Yours faithfully, E Saunders (Superintendent).*

And again: *Dear Miss Davies . . . 15th October . . . failed to take back your child . . . In absence of any formal application . . .*

October. The six months had been calculated from the day when the contract was signed. She'd not understood, that's all. It was just a mistake, a simple mistake. She could tell Mrs Saunders she'd got it wrong, explain to her that –

'Seeing Tom's not coming out today, can you take me with you instead?' Donna was tugging at her sleeve. 'We could go to the canal, if you like. See the ducks. Last week I saw four of them when—'

She'd thought it was six months from the day when Tom first came to the home. From *October* 1949, Tom wasn't even born then. How could they – ?

'I need to see Mrs Saunders.'

'Mrs Saunders isn't here. They said to say she's having dinner with the Government.'

The second paragraph was one short sentence. She had to

read the words several times over: '*From the date of this letter, no further access to your child will be permitted.*'

No further access . . .

No further access . . .

No further access . . .

Donna was tugging at her sleeve. 'So can we go to the canal?'

'Tom *is* here, isn't he? You've seen him?'

'They said to tell you he's got a bit of a cold and he's getting better now, like I said. He's maybe sleeping.' Donna was trying to take hold of her hand now. 'The canal. Please, Miss Davies, please.'

Maggie took a step forward and pushed at the part-opened door. It was being jammed from behind.

'Donna. Indoors, now!' Boss Beryl stood in the doorway.

'Bye, Miss Davies. Maybe we can see the ducks another time?' With a cheerful wave, Donna stretched up onto her tip-toes and then ballet-stepped gracefully back into the hall.

'Mrs Saunders isn't here, Miss Davies, and the letter explains the situation.' Boss Beryl tried to push the door shut.

Maggie stuck her foot in the gap. 'Is Tom all right?'

'Please remove your foot, Miss Davies.'

'Is Tom all right? I want to know. This letter says—'

'Remove your foot and I'll tell you.'

Beryl opened the door a crack wider . . . and the instant Maggie withdrew her foot the door was slammed in her face. She heard the key turn.

Maggie stared at the locked door. If only she'd not spoken to the superintendent the day before. If only she'd not said a word to anyone, just taken Tom for his walk, same as usual, then simply kept on walking. He was her own child so it couldn't be stealing, surely?

She made a complete circuit of the house – all the windows were closed, all the doors locked. When she rapped on the playroom window, some of the older children saw her and waved back. The staff ignored her. There was no sign of Donna. Then, one by one, all the downstairs curtains were drawn shut. The building had been made into a fortified castle.

Twice she went round it.

Having returned to the front door she gave the bell pull another tug – firmly but not too strong. Not wanting to wake the wee ones who'd already be in bed, not wanting to upset anyone, not wanting to make a scene. All she wanted was to see Tom, to know that he was safe and –

Another tug at the bell.

Not a sound this time.

She tugged again.

And again.

The bell pull had gone completely slack, its brass handle no longer sliding smoothly back into the wall.

Hanging loosely on its wire.

Disconnected? Did they really think a disconnected bell would would stop her? That she'd simply give up and walk away?

She crouched down and began calling through the letter-box, loudly as she dared: 'Beryl! Mrs Saunders!'

'Stop that row!' Boss Beryl was right behind the door.

'Let me see TOM!'

The response was immediate. 'Stop your shouting! You'll frighten the children!'

'Open the door then. Please.'

'We'll call the police.'

'No – I only want to see Tom, and to know he's okay. That's all. I don't want any trouble.'

She waited.

'Talk to me face to face at least.'

She waited longer.

Then, after several seconds, Beryl's voice came back to her: 'All right. But you have to stand clear first. Then I'll open it.'

Maggie took an immediate step back. 'I'm standing away.'

As soon as she heard the key turning in the lock, she prepared herself.

She watched the door ease open an inch at a time.

Boss Beryl faced her through the tiny gap. 'You're still too close, Miss Davies.'

Without taking her eyes off Beryl, Maggie took another step back. 'Far enough?'

She focused on the crack she could see widening between the door and its frame. She tensed herself. She was ready. She knew she would only have the one chance.

'Is Tom with you?'

'No, he's fast aslee—'

Lunging suddenly forward, her whole weight shouldering the door –

Boss Beryl tried to stand firm, but was too late.

Maggie shoved her aside, then rushed across the hall and bounded up the stairs three steps at a time. A group of younger children, some holding hands, stood on the landing, one of them calling out, 'Mummy! Mummy!' at the top of his voice.

'Sshhh! It's okay, it's okay. Shh! I'm here to see Tom.'

Boss Beryl came hurrying after.

'Stop! You can't just barge your way in. Mrs Saunders said that—'

Next moment she was in Tom's dormitory, Boss Beryl calling behind her:

'What do you think you're doing? Get back downstairs at once.'

Maggie headed across to the far corner. Past Crib Number 8. Crib Number 9 . . .

'Mrs Saunders said that if you came . . .'

. . . Crib 10 . . . Crib 11 –

'. . . I was to tell you that—'

Crib 11 was empty. Tom's crib was empty.

She snatched up the patchwork blanket, pressing it to her face. Tom's blanket.

'Where is he? Where is he?'

SUNDAY

'Finish, Mrs Stewart?' Donna's come to take away your tray.

That lass had better take care she doesn't let herself go, helping herself to a chocolate biscuit every time she gets a chance . . . She'll never become a chorus girl gorging herself like that.

'Where's all the photos, Mum? There's nothing here.'

You watch him turn over blank page after blank page until he comes to the only photograph left in the album.

'Who's that?'

'Donna, of course.' You smile at the would-be dancer as she lifts away the tray. 'Before she discovered chocolate biscuits. Am I right?'

The young Polish woman squints at the photo. 'Nice baby, Mrs Stewart. I come soon with meds. Bye, Mrs Stewart.'

'But, Mum, you can't be meaning someone *here*, in Rosehaven? This is just a wee girl – it's an old black & white photo, must have been taken over fifty years ago! The pram's like something out of a museum. How can it be the Polish woman here, the one you call Donna? And what's happened to the rest of the photos?'

You shrug again. All these questions. Like someone

turning the wringer, wanting to get all the water squeezed out. But there's hardly a drop left, is there?

Managing without anyone's help, you slide the photo out of its plastic sleeve. 'That's my little boy. He's called Tom.'

'Tom? But I'm—'

'Ssh! It's a secret, remember. But he's being well looked after. Donna treats him like a wee brother.'

'I don't understand, Mum.'

'Sssh! I know what: you take it, you can look after it for me. Things vanish here sometimes.'

He keeps saying he doesn't understand and you keep insisting. Finally he gives you a nod. 'If you're sure that's what you want,' and he slips Tom's photo into his jacket pocket. 'It'll be safe now.'

You smile at each other. For once, something feels right.

With your visitor gone, the sun'll be on the move again. And so . . .

Zimmering full-speed out of your bedroom door, down the corridor, round the corner, across the hall and into the dayroom. Your usual seat in its usual place in the line against the wall. You sit down just in time. Closing your eyes, you feel the sun edging its way onto your cheek. Its warmth flowing across your face, your eyelids, your cheeks, touching your lips, your neck . . . soaking into you.

More. More. You want more. You want to feel that warmth flooding into you, drenching your whole body.

Take care – if you open your eyes too soon, you'll find yourself back in the dayroom.

The sun is all that matters now, holding you safe and

secure before it moves on. Till then, you can give yourself completely to its touch, its warm and loving touch. Like Michael's. These sighs of contentment are the thanks you offer in return.

7

STANDING MOTIONLESS BESIDE Tom's empty cot, her face buried in his patchwork quilt, breathing in his baby-smell. Drawing in its sweetness, breathing it deep inside her . . .

Then she felt the touch of someone's hand on her shoulder.

'It's all right, Miss Davies. Tom's fine. Your wee boy's fine.' Boss Beryl had switched to professional calm – pitched low, her voice set at sympathy-and-concern tone. The reassuring smile seemed genuine: 'Don't worry, Miss Davies. Really. Everything's been taken care of and couldn't be better. Tom's fine and in good hands. No need to distress yourself.' Boss Beryl crossed to the nearest cot and picked up a swaddled bundle that was clearly on the point of turning into a swollen-faced, full-volume, red scream and began rocking the baby in her arms. *'There, there, sweetie. Nothing to worry about. Everyone's going sleepy-byes . . .'*

Maggie clutched the patchwork blanket to her chest. 'Where is he? Where's Tom?'

'Arthur's Seat, I think they said.'

'Arthur's Seat?' Maggie glanced towards the window. 'I don't understand. What's he doing there? Who's *they*, and why—?'

'It's okay, Miss Davies, really. Calm down. Lucky boy's been having himself a day out.'

'He's coming back?'

'Of course.'

'When?'

'Or maybe it was Princes Street Gardens they said? A chance for him to hear the band. A day out, like I said. He'll have had a whale of a time, you can count on it.' She reached to take the blanket. 'This his? I'll put it in the wash. Thanks.'

Maggie's grip on the patchwork tightened. 'When's he coming back?'

'Keep your voice down, Miss Davies.'

'No one told me anything. Not a word.'

'Maybe they should've. Bit of a shock, I suppose. But . . . well, it had to happen one day. Children don't stay here for ever.'

'He *is* coming back?'

'Yes. But Mrs Saunders says that seeing you've not managed to—'

'I told her that this weekend I was—'

'I'm very sorry, Miss Davies, and I wish I could help you.' Boss Beryl shook her head and again reached for the blanket. 'I really do.'

Maggie's fingers kept firm hold of the patchwork. 'Mrs Saunders can't just *give* him away.'

'Keep your voice down.'

'Don't you tell me what to do. I've done everything I can. Everything. And now he's being stolen from—'

The petrol pump took a step back. 'No one's stealing him. He'll be coming back, I tell you.'

'When?'

'Mrs Saunders says—'

'I couldn't care less about Mrs Saunders.' She advanced on Boss Beryl. 'When? I asked you when will my son be brought back?'

'No idea. I don't know. No one tells me. I don't do the office stuff.'

No idea? Without meaning to, Maggie ripped the small patchwork quilt in two and then, the torn pieces still in her hands, she all but collapsed against the empty cot. She was suddenly exhausted.

'I'll wait for him.'

'Suit yourself – but you'll not be waiting in here. *Everything's okay, little one. Close your sleepy eyes and . . .* Mrs Saunders is at a Governors' dinner this evening. Your best plan's to give her a phone first thing Monday morning.'

'But what am I to do? That letter says that I'm not allowed to—'

'Look, Miss Davies, I've got my hands full here. If it was up to me . . .' She shrugged. 'Drop her a line's my advice.' She laid the now sleeping child down on its mattress. *'Back to bed, sweetie. Sleepy heads, sleepy beds, sleepy, sleepy sleep . . .'*

Arthur's Seat? Princes St Gardens? A chance to hear the band . . . ? Was the whole city of Edinburgh betraying her? Maggie turned and stumbled out of the room.

Spending the day with strangers, and the evening too. Having a whale of a time with strangers. Strangers holding him in their arms. Strangers making him smile and laugh . . .

The wooden banister . . . then down the staircase, tread after wearying tread . . . the empty hall.

She sat down in the carved wooden chair, the torn pieces of Tom's patchwork blanket on her lap. Not even strength enough to cross her legs.

Quarter-of-an-hour later Boss Beryl came down carrying a bundle of dirty sheets.

'You still here?'

'I'm waiting for Tom.'

Boss Beryl snorted, and continued down the basement stairs. When she returned a short time later she crossed the hall to Mrs Saunders' office, closing the door behind her. Maggie heard her speaking on the phone but couldn't make out the words. A few moments later she was back.

'I'm sorry, Miss Davies, but you'll have to wait outside. You're a disturbance.'

'What? I'm not disturbing anybody. I'm not leaving till I see—'

'And now you've received Mrs Saunders' letter, you're trespassing. That's the law. Do I have to call the police?'

Up and down the short stretch of pavement outside the home, up and down in the gathering darkness. Eventually letting herself back into the garden to sit on the bench next to the sandpit with its tumbled remains of a bucket-and-spade castle, its trampled-down battlements. She was careful to keep watch on the street, but no cars stopped. No one came to the house, no one left. From time to time a tram rumbled past. At ten o'clock she saw the upstairs lights being switched on and off as the staff made their final rounds.

At ten-thirty the last light went out – everyone had gone to bed.

§

Next day was Saturday. Come lunchtime, Maggie hurried out of Blair & Blair's and up the street to the Hanover Street PO phone box.

No reply – Jean probably wasn't at the bakery this weekend. She pressed button B and her pennies clattered back to her.

Which left her parents.

Her parents. Their ignoring her, cutting her dead as she'd stood there in front them – the knitting needles' relentless *click-clicking*, the stripped-out bedroom upstairs. Like she'd never even existed.

Mrs Melville would have talked, though. Her mother would have listened. Tom was her own grandson, after all.

It was worth a try. She was going to need all the help she could get.

She dropped in the coins once more and dialled Newhaven.

As it rang, she pictured the telephone receiver on the hall table with the oval mirror above, and the silenced grandfather clock standing nearby.

Her father answered. She hung up.

Maggie made two trips to Woodstock House that afternoon and three on Sunday, each time finding the front door firmly locked. The bell hadn't been re-connected and the only response to her frantic knocking was to see either Boss Beryl or Donna appear at one of the windows. Boss Beryl would jerk her arm from side to side, gesturing at her to go away; Donna would give her a friendly wave and remain standing at the window until she left.

First thing Monday morning before work, Maggie phoned Jean from the Hanover Street call box.

'Lucky to catch me in, Maggie. I was picking up a cake I've made for the folks we'll be staying with. We're just off.'

'Jean, they've stopped me seeing Tom. Mrs Saunders' letter says that—'

Jean was really, really sorry but she had to dash. She and Billy were going away for a few days. Been arranged ages ago. She'd be back late on Friday. After Maggie had finished work on Saturday they could go together to Woodstock House and –

'But they won't let us in. Saunders' letter says that I can't—'

Jean was so, so sorry. How could they? That was awful. Really terrible. But she had to go. She just had to. Billy was waiting for her on the platform and she was already late. If they missed that train . . . Maggie mustn't lose heart, mustn't give up. She would be in her thoughts all week. And Tom, too.

They said goodbye.

Maggie checked her appearance in the mirror of her compact. She waited, dabbing her eyes. She now had to go to work. Nothing of the distress tearing her apart must show, nothing must betray her.

For the next few days Maggie hardly ate or slept. Before work, during her lunch break, and after work she'd ring the children's home. When Old Woodbine was out of the office, she sometimes even risked using the phone on the older woman's desk. The instant she heard her returning along the corridor, she hung up and hurried back to her own seat.

She was told that Mrs Saunders wasn't in.

She was told to please wait, Mrs Saunders would come to

the phone shortly.

She was told that Mrs Saunders would return later in the morning / later in the afternoon / first thing next day.

She was told that Mrs Saunders knew she'd been trying to get hold of her and would be sure to be in touch.

She was always asked to leave her number.

Leave her number? Forget it. For even if Mrs Saunders did phone her back – which Maggie was certain she never would – then Old Woodbine would take the call . . . and that would be that. Mr Blair was a kindly man – he might be the boss, but he wasn't in charge. Old Woodbine sharing an office with *an unmarried mother*? Blair & Blair letters typed on a Blair & Blair typewriter by *an unmarried mother*? Blair & Blair clients being exposed to the risk of having contact with *an unmarried mother*? No chance, not in a million years. The first hint of her having an illegitimate child hidden away somewhere, and Old Woodbine would have her sacked on the spot. She'd be shown the street door so fast her feet wouldn't even touch the stairs on the way down.

She wrote three letters to the superintendent, each more desperate than the last.

Her first received an immediate response – a copy of the letter she'd already been given.

Her second – no reply.

Her third – no reply.

She wrote to Michael. She told him everything, said her life was falling apart, said she couldn't sleep for worrying she might lose Tom, might never see him again . . . They'd stopped her. Everything was locked. And he wasn't there. They were giving him to strangers. She was his mother. If that happened

. . . she couldn't go on living . . . couldn't bear it. Page after page, it was a frantic outpouring of frustration and rage, of despair. She received Michael's reply by return, on the Saturday morning.

Was Old Woodbine never going to move, was she going to remain glued to her chair all morning? Not until nearly 11.00 did the older woman get up and leave the room.

The instant she was alone Maggie crossed to the other desk and phoned Jean. Her sister-in-law was in.

'Thank God, I've caught you, Jean. It's Michael. I'm at my wits' end. I don't know what I'm going to . . . Can I come round and—?'

'I'll be here all day, Maggie. Take it easy. You can tell me when you get—'

Hearing Old Woodbine coming back along the corridor, Maggie hung up.

From then on, the hands of the office clock slowed down to quarter speed.

At last she was on the tram. Standing room only, all the way to Dalry Road. She leapt off well before it stopped, ran across the street, straight up to Jean's, and in her front door. Not even pausing to say hello –

'He's coming to Edinburgh.'

Only when she'd said the words out loud did she herself really take them in: Michael. In Edinburgh.

'He's whit?'

'Arriving late tonight.'

'Tae rescue ye, like a knight on a white horse? A white stick mair like—'

'Wants us to get married.'

Jean picked up the phone: 'Ring him. Tell him tae—'

'Too late. He's already on his way. Morning ferry, then the train. Lachlan's bringing him here.'

'Tae the bakery?'

'He said he knew he couldn't just turn up at Mrs Mc-Cann's, so I'm to meet him here tonight at 11.' She trailed off in embarrassment: 'He wasn't sure how the trains would work out . . .'

'He can stay a few days, Maggie, but that's aa. I canna dae mair, it's just no—'

'I'm sorry, Jean. I'm so sorry, I'm sorry . . .' She collapsed onto the chair with her head in her hands. Then she told her sister-in-law about trying to phone Mrs Saunders and writing letters. 'I'm going to lose Tom. I'm going to lose him, Jean. What'll I do?'

'Dinna tak on, lass. Dinna greet.'

Maggie felt the older woman's arms round her, and her hand stroking her hair.

'I'm sorry tae,' Jean whispered. 'Oh, Maggie – it's twae bairns ye'll hae nou.'

'But I love him. I love them both.'

'Richt enough, but Tom's the yin as needs ye maist. Tom needs ye. Forget Mrs Saunders, forget writing her letters and phoning and leaving messages. Forget playing by their rules, Maggie. Ye'll only lose – that's whit rules are fer.'

'And so?'

'Play tae yer strengths. *We*'ll play tae *oor* strengths. Mrs Saunders will be away fer a lang weekend, ye said? Okay –

it's nou or never.' Her sister-in-law stood up. 'Come on, we've work tae dae.'

It was evening when the two women climbed out of the taxi. Side by side they marched up the front steps of Woodstock House.

Once it was explained that they'd come to hand over a present for the staff, a token of Maggie's appreciation for all their good work when looking after Tom, they were let in.

The shiny pink box, tied with the showy gold ribbon that Jean had curled at the ends, was placed on the kitchen table. It looked a very special gift indeed. When it was unwrapped, there were genuine gasps as the lid was raised to reveal a triple-layered, mouth-watering masterpiece of chocolate, cream and marzipan that had been showered in multi-coloured hundreds-and-thousands. Quite clearly the ration book had been thrown out the window. THANK YOU was spelled out in red icing. Thick slices were cut and handed round.

Everything was going to plan, and so Maggie asked if she might go upstairs for one last look at her wee boy?

There was an embarrassed silence.

'I won't wake him or pick him up.'

More silence.

Boss Beryl finished swallowing down a mouthful of cake: 'I'm afraid that's not possible. Mrs Saunders has made it quite clear that—'

'Mrs Saunders isn't here.'

'I am her representative. Myself, I'd like to let you see him, Miss Davies, really I would, but—'

'Come on,' interrupted Jean. 'Yin last look at her bairn,

for God's sake. Just because yer boss is a wee Hitler disnae mak you yin. Maggie winna even touch him – aa richt? Ye can gang up wi her. I'll stay here – guard yer next slice for ye.'

Seeing Tom lying there asleep in his crib, Maggie broke down and cried as if her heart would burst. While Boss Beryl looked on, she sobbed and sobbed. She couldn't help it. No pretence needed, these were real tears. Maggie knew that if things didn't work out this might very well be the last time she would see Tom. She was so upset she nearly had Boss Beryl in tears as well. Finally, though, she mastered herself and begged to be allowed to kiss him a final goodbye.

Afterwards, wiping her eyes clear, she turned and stumbled out of the room.

Down in the hall, Boss Beryl laid a hand on her arm, adding that she was so very sorry that everything had ended like this. Maggie should rest assured Tom would be well looked after, he'd be brought up in a good home with a loving family who could provide the best for him. Mrs Saunders was a really kind woman and always had the children's best interests at heart. Maggie nodded, then asked if she could use the toilet before they left. Boss Beryl remained waiting outside until Maggie had finished, and then escorted her back to the kitchen.

Five minutes later Maggie and Jean said their goodbyes and left.

Now they had to go their separate ways – Jean to the bakery to wait for Michael's arrival, Maggie to Glengyle Terrace to make the necessary preparations. By ten-thirty she had everything ready. It was too early to return to Woodstock House, but there wasn't enough time to go all the way to the bakery and be there to greet Michael.

Michael. How she longed to see him. Nearly a whole year's longing. And in less than a couple of hours . . .

Things would work out, they *had* to. She'd done everything she could. Now she needed to wait. That was all.

So she put on her coat and outdoor shoes, and sat on the edge of her bed. Waiting. A few minutes later she was up again, pacing the room. Then back on the bed, only to get up and start pacing all over again . . .

'It was nearly 11 when Maggie pulled the front door shut behind her, went down the steps and across to the park. Late April perhaps, but it looked and felt like the darkest night of the year. Not a star in the sky and a dampness and heaviness in the air that threatened rain, and lots of it. Good. It would keep people off the street.

She stepped lively – across Bruntsfield Links, past the unlit shops and silent tenements to Holy Corner. The only sound was her own footsteps.

If she wanted, she could turn round at any moment and go straight to the bakery instead. No harm done. She would marry Michael, set up home and then Mrs Saunders would surely let her keep Tom. She would have to. She *would*. Surely.

But by then it might all be too late.

Maggie kept walking. The first drops of rain began to fall

as she turned off Morningside Road. A glance at her watch, plenty of time.

She didn't trust Mrs Saunders. It was as simple as that.

By the time the outline of the children's home loomed up in the darkness, the rain was coming down in torrents. Not a single light showed. Maggie checked her watch again – she'd made good time and now had exactly thirty-five minutes. She pushed open the gate.

Of course you can't come, too, Jean. I'll need someone to visit me in jail! she'd joked as they'd said goodbye. But it was no joke now.

She paused for a moment on the wet path, drenched through and almost blinded by the driving rain. This was her last chance to turn back. If she was caught and sent to prison, then Tom would be lost to her for ever.

But as things were, she'd already lost him. So what real choice had she?

Next moment she was squelching across the lawn.

Having reached the rear of the building, she flashed her torch quickly round the cement yard till she found a pile of discarded wooden boxes stacked at the side of a small outhouse. An orange crate looked the sturdiest. More or less intact and the wood slimy with rain, it was probably strong enough to take her weight. She returned to the back wall – another flash of her torch located what she was looking for, the window with frosted glass. She positioned the box beneath it.

Holding onto the window ledge for support, clambering up. Standing there for a moment to get her balance, wobbling slightly. A tentative half-rocking from side to side on her feet to test it. The box held.

So far so good.

Now for the tricky part. Both hands pressed against the sides of the window frame, she pushed upwards.

Nothing happened. Not the slightest give.

Pushed again.

She paused to wipe the rain from her eyes, then pushed even harder . . .

Not too hard though. The window had to be *eased* open ever so slowly. Eased open noiselessly.

She pushed . . . and pushed . . . and pushed. It was the toilet window all right, the one she'd unsnibbed a few hours earlier, but someone must have re-snibbed it.

After all their careful planning . . . She stopped herself from screaming out loud.

For several seconds she remained standing on the box, hands on the wooden sill, struggling to hold back her tears, resisting putting her fist through the window.

At last she stepped down and carried the box along to the next window. If she had to, she'd work her way right round the house. Having come this far, what else could she do?

Clambering up again at the next window. Then the next after that. Her hands pressed against the frame . . .

Starting to push upwards . . .

Third time lucky! It slid open easily. The wood screeched. She froze.

Remained standing motionless for as long as she could bear, the rain lashing down onto her head, shoulders and back . . . She forced herself not to move. Fist clenched, she counted under her breath, ready to jump clear and make a run for it at the first sign of a light going on, or at the sounds of someone coming.

Nineteen, twenty. She relaxed, inched the window up enough to let her climb through . . . Moments later she was standing in Mrs Saunders' office. Perfect.

There was even a towel provided, a pair of towels, in fact – rust-red, extra thick and long. Having wiped some of the rain from her hands and face, she closed the curtains and switched on her torch. A glance at her watch – twenty-two minutes left. She and Jean had debated what she should do next – secure the paperwork first, or go straight upstairs? There'd be masses of files and she'd no idea how long she'd take to find what she was looking for.

She had to speed up.

The metal filing cabinet wasn't locked. Good.

Top drawer – *Adoptions*. The files each had a tab and were arranged by date. Good again. Most recent at the front – Montrose, Iris. 3/12/50. Next was Watson, James. 28/11/50. No mention of any adoption involving Tom. She breathed out a sigh of relief and slid the drawer back into place.

The one beneath was labelled *Admissions*.

She riffled through the files . . . 12/12/50 . . . 18/11/50 . . . 3/10/50 . . . 25/9/50 . . . to reach those further at the back. About three-quarters in, she came across the tab marked '17/11/49 – Davies, Tom.' Her hands shook as she pulled out the file.

She laid the folder on Mrs Saunders' desk and, by torchlight, turned over the few pages of Tom's short life. Even though she was in a hurry, she flicked through the sheets to check everything was there – his birth certificate, the letter from the Queen's Crescent nursing home and the doctor's notes, the detested contract she'd signed and the various other forms Mrs Saunders had made her complete. Her own details were also included: Jean's bakery address had been scored out and replaced by Glengyle Terrace. A handwritten note was attached: *Father probably still married*. There was a copy of the letter denying her access and her own unanswered replies, also the photo she herself had taken of Donna and Tom beside the Tractor. In addition, a sheaf of papers clipped together was headed: *Adoption – Interest*. Promising herself to burn these unread, she stuffed the complete file under her jersey and pushed the drawer shut. Good – there'd be no tell-tale paperwork left behind.

Another glance at her watch – only eighteen minutes left. She switched off the torch and stepped into the hall. It was in complete darkness. Above her, she could hear the rain hammering onto the glass cupola. Making sure she didn't blunder into the wooden throne or the Tractor, she crossed to the vestibule. A quick flash of the torch located the key, she turned it slowly to unlock the front door. No top and bottom bolts, thank goodness. Back to the hall. If it had been a clear night there would have been enough light to see her way upstairs. But it really was pitch black.

Keeping the torch beam pointed down at her feet, she began climbing the stairs, holding on to the banister in the darkness.

Halfway up, one of the boards creaked underfoot. She froze. Switched off her torch. Stopped breathing.

Began counting into herself as slowly as she dared. *One, two, three . . .*

She stood motionless, straining to hear the slightest sign

that someone ... *eight ... nine ... ten ... eleven ...*

At full alert, rigid, peering into the darkness ... *fourteen, fifteen ...*

Then she relaxed.

Placed her foot down gradually, very, very gradually. Letting the next step take her weight slowly, steadily ...

Again she held her breath.

Nothing.

The next tread. Pressing lightly as she could. A little more, a little more ... The only sound was the rain gusting heavier every few seconds against the cupola. She continued up to the top.

Fifteen minutes left.

From along the corridor came the rasp-and-snort of someone snoring. Boss Beryl? She certainly hoped so.

Time began speeding up. Keeping the torch beam directed at the floor, she inched open the door and stepped into Tom's dormitory. Tiptoeing across the room, slowly, carefully. Watching out for the table that stood in the middle, and for any pails or –

One of the babies was gurgling to itself, clearly awake. Another was standing up in its cot and stared at her as she passed.

'Ssssh! Little one. Please don't ... don't ...'

The baby blinked, reached out its small hand and started to whimper.

'No .. no. Please, please no. *Sssssh!*'

Then, a moment later, it slid down flat again on its mattress and closed its eyes.

Maggie let out a breath she hadn't realised she'd been

holding in. Like crossing a minefield, she thought. She reached cot number 11.

Tom was fast asleep, wrapped in a new blanket and with one of Donkey Boy's floppy ears clutched in his tight little fist. He looked perfectly content.

He was usually wide awake when she visited. Not like this, lying here so peacefully, safe and secure in his familiar surroundings. She knew she was about to disrupt all that. She'd be wrenching him away from everything he had ever known in his brief life, destroying a carefully planned future. Other people's good intentions, other people's plans.

She could still turn back now, creep off down the stairs and walk out the front door. But then what?

The pendulum she'd thrown into the glass-green water and had imagined sinking deeper and deeper into the harbour – would that be her? Without Tom, what would the days and years ahead be but a hopeless choking slide into ever-deepening mud?

Next moment she'd lifted him out of the crib.

He didn't even wake.

She closed the dormitory door behind her.

Out in the corridor she paused. Something seemed different from before. The complete silence. It had stopped raining. Moonlight was beginning to filter down from the cupola.

She switched off the torch and, treading even more carefully, made her way along the corridor. Already she could make out the silhouettes of a fire bucket, a side table, picture frames. The top of the stairs only a few steps away.

'Miss Davies?'

She stopped. Utterly. Rigid.

A faint shimmer of whiteness up ahead. A whispered voice: 'Miss Davies?'

'Ssh, Donna!' Maggie hissed and put a finger to her lips.

'You've got Tom with you?'

'Ssh!' Maggie stood beside her at the top of stairs. 'Donna, please. Ssh!'

'Take me, too.'

The moonlight was getting stronger. The future chorus-girl was in a long white nightdress and bare feet, her hair sleep-tangled. 'Please, Miss Davies, please.'

What if she just shoved Donna out of the way and rushed down the stairs without stopping, then ran out the front door and off up the street? Everything might still be all right. She had all the official records with her, and she had Tom. But she'd have to do it *now*.

Maggie shook her head and tried to push past.

The girl didn't budge: 'If you don't take me, I'll scream as loud as I can and wake everyone.' She stretched her arms out wide, barring Maggie's way down.

Tom had started fidgeting in his sleep, his small feet pressed into her stomach and his head shifted from side to side as if he might wake at any moment.

'Please, Donna. You don't understand. Let me past. I have to take Tom and—'

'I don't care,' the young girl whispered. 'Take me—'

A door opened at the end of the corridor. 'Who's there?'

It was Boss Beryl. Maggie clutched Tom to her chest.

'It's just me, Mrs Ferguson.' Donna replied in her normal voice. 'Needed the toilet. Very sorry for waking you.'

'I've told you before about drinking water last thing at night, Donna. Be as quiet as you can and then straight back to bed. Goodnight.' The door closed.

Maggie whispered, 'Thank you, Donna.'

'Give me Tom.'

'What?'

'I need to get dressed and I'm not letting you leave without me. Give him here.' She held out her hands. 'If you don't, I'll scream. I mean it.'

Maggie hesitated.

'I will, Miss Davies. I will. Really.'

Donna occupied an attic room up a flight of narrow, uncarpeted stairs – more like a walk-in cupboard with a bed under the sloping ceiling. Maggie watched her get dressed. Only eight minutes remained.

'Donna, you must understand that—'

'I'm ready now, Miss Davies. Let's go.'

Without answering, Maggie laid Tom down carefully on the girl's bed.

'Listen, Donna . . .'

She grabbed the girl by the shoulders and leant into her face. 'You can't come with us. You can't. Understand?'

Struggling and kicking out to free herself, the girl jerked to one side as if she was about to call for help. Instantly Maggie clamped a hand over her mouth.

'You try coming with us and I'll get rid of you,' she hissed into the child's ear. 'They'll think you ran off during the night, taking Tom with you.'

'But that's not what—'

Maggie clamped her hand harder.

'The police'll hunt you down and when they find you alone and *without* Tom – he and I will be long gone by then – they'll think you *killed* him.'

'Mmmmmm . . .'

'People do that sometimes, you know, kill children.'

'But I wouldn't – mmmmm . . .'

'They'll hang you, Donna.'

'Nooo – mmmm . . .'

'The rope'll go tighter and tighter round your neck until you can't breathe, till your eyes burst, till your tongue turns black. Understand?' She ignored the terror she could see in the girl's face. 'Do you want that?'

Donna shook her head.

'If you scream for help now, I'll run and I'll get away.' Maggie paused, then stared deep into the girl's eyes. 'I'll return one night soon, just like I did tonight. And I'll creep up these stairs, like I did tonight. I'll come here, right into your room while you're asleep . . . and snap your neck. Understand?'

The girl nodded. She'd started to cry.

'So then, are you going to scream?'

Donna shook her head.

'Good girl.' Maggie began loosening her grip.

'You won't take me with you – ever?'

'I can't. I'm really sorry, Donna. I'd like to, but I just can't.' Then she added. 'Maybe once we're settled we can meet one day and—'

'I hate you!' Wiping the tears with the back of her hand

'Donna—'

'I hate you. I hate you.' The girl threw herself onto her

bed, burying her face in the pillow.

Maggie reached down to stroke the tangle of curls, then stopped herself. She sighed, picked up Tom, and left the room.

Clutching Tom in her arms, Maggie paced up and down the short stretch of pavement where the taxi was supposed to meet her. Past low stone walls stripped of their iron railings; past high stone walls still streaming wet in the streetlight; past gates locked for the night: past trees whose branches thrashed the darkness. Three, four times she walked to the red pillar box at the next corner, turned and came back again. Up and down, up and down with hardly a pause. She'd got there only a couple of minutes after midnight. Maybe the taxi had arrived and, seeing no one waiting, had driven off? But then where was Jean? Michael?

At every turn she glanced back down the street towards the children's home, terrified she'd see lights and hear people shouting. Woodstock House, however, remained in darkness. Remained silent. She was ashamed at the way she'd threatened Donna. But what else could she have done?

Halting several times in mid-stride – was that the clanging of a police bell? Was a squad car about to come screeching round the corner?

Twice she saw headlights approaching from Bruntsfield, only to watch the car drive straight past. The only sound was rainwater gushing out of a blocked gutter nearby, splashing down onto someone's front step.

Once again she walked to the pillar box and back, singing under her breath:

My Baby Bunting,

Daddy's gone a-hunting,
To catch a baby rabbit's skin
To wrap our –

At last – another set of headlights, and coming from the right direction. It was slowing down. A taxi. *Their* taxi. Had to be.

The black cab drew up beside her, the driver's window was lowered:

'Sorry I'm late, Missus. Engine kept needing cranked up. Doesn't like getting up this early on a Sunday morning!'

Jean was sitting in the back. She was alone.

Maggie climbed in. 'But where's –?'

'Dinna fear, Maggie, Michael's back at the bakery. He's waiting fer ye.'

SUNDAY MORNING

An axe to the worn-out dining chairs. Slice and dice. Turn carpentry to kindling and haul the smashed woodwork in armfuls out to the garden and up the path to the heaped bonfire. Dragging the fifties' kitchen cabinet that even the charity shop didn't want. The three-legged stool you used to stand on when your mother did the washing, the rickety hat stand, wooden clothes-horse, bits of smashed shelving – worthless junk the lot of it, good only for burning.

You'll keep these photographs of your mother, of course – in her wellingtons boots digging up potatoes, dressed up smart for a trip to Edinburgh, and some others. The rest are a load of strangers and there's no one to tell you who they were. Back in the black-and-white past, people hoarded their photos. Not like today's disposable memories – the freeze-framed smiles, drunken moonies, drunken meals, the googled Earth itself. Everyone's life Photoshopped to perfection for posting on Facebook or YouTube. The moment's been saved . . . then so are you?

Not really. But getting there.

A nice one of Auntie Jean. That smoky voice of hers and her tobacco-smelling clothes – the only relative you ever met and then only for afternoon tea and cakes in Mackie's. Never visited her home. Seems there was an Uncle Billy, not that you ever met him. Never asked why. This soldier standing next to a signpost pointing to Berlin – is that your Uncle Billy? Your mother won't remember, that's for sure. And so – in goes Mr Berlin, along with all the others.

But you have tried. Making that album for her, hoping she'll talk you through the photos. Would be nice to learn more about her life and about your dad, more than that he was blind and got knocked down by an Edinburgh tram when you were very young. Talking about the past makes her sad, she says.

Which leaves that snap she gave you, the one of the little girl standing next to a big old-fashioned pram, holding somebody's baby in her arms. A neighbour? A girl in the village? No idea. Might as well go in, too.

And so – pour on the paraffin, toss on the lighted match. *Whoosh!* Cremation of a sort.

They're gone in seconds.

Time for a final walk through the cleared-out cottage. No curtains, no lampshades, empty grates; kitchen shelves and windowsills stripped bare. Without furniture, the walls look grimy, the woodwork's badly scuffed, the paintwork chipped. No retro charm here, the buyer'll start by ripping out that monstrosity of a pre-war fireplace. Ghosts are already haunting the place: the pale after-images on the walls where your mother's pictures hung, the outlines of her kitchen cabinet and dresser, her wardrobe. The lino's scarred where you dragged out the cooker, the fridge and washing machine – three veterans fit only for recycling at the Council dump. Easy to imagine hearing your mother's voice here – from the time when she still knew who you were, of course. Maybe her footsteps will echo in the empty rooms? Yours, too?

No . . . not a sound in the place. Your long-ago childhood home. Empty. Hollowed-out. You lock the door behind you. The bonfire can be left to burn itself out.

8

THE NEXT FORTNIGHT passed very quickly, and happily. Maggie explained to Sheila that she'd had a big row with her mother about turning up like that and wanting to take Tom away for the weekend. If everything worked out, she'd asked, could he now stay at Glengyle Terrace?

'Let's see how we get on,' had been her landlady's response.

Luckily they got on very well. For a little extra on the rent Sheila agreed to look after Tom during the day, which allowed Maggie to continue working at Blair & Blair's. On her part, Maggie was available evenings and weekends, if required, to look after both boys. They'd soon settled into a routine.

It would have been too much of a coincidence if Michael had turned up completely cured on the very same day she brought her baby home, so it was decided that he should remain at the bakery for a little longer. Maggie visited him as often as possible, Jean taking Tom out in the pram to give them privacy.

'My husband's really starting to respond,' Maggie told Sheila one morning. 'The doctors say we might soon have him home.'

Everything seemed to be working out. For the first few days Maggie had jumped to her feet in alarm whenever she heard the doorbell – perhaps in her haste at Woodstock House she'd overlooked something that could be used to trace her? Again and again she went over in her mind the paperwork she'd found in Tom's file. His birth certificate, her signed contract, various letters. That would be everything, surely? But were there duplicates somewhere?

After a week, however, she began to relax. The week then became a fortnight.

On the first Saturday in June, nearly a year to the day she'd stepped off the ferry at Stornoway and been directed to Mrs Stewart's lodging house, Maggie hesitated outside the street door in Glengyle Terrace. Michael was beside her. Never had she felt so nervous.

'It's blue,' she said. 'A shiny blue door, with a brass handle and a letter box.' She wanted to say how wonderful it was to have him here at last, how this was the beginning of their life together. 'Here's our key, I'll let us in.'

She went in and Michael followed. Once inside, she couldn't seem to stop.

'There's a long hall with a table for letters and things. Mrs McCann's put some welcome flowers on it for you. Sun-yellow, pink and white. Ones you can smell. Freesias, I think.' She brought him up to the vase. 'As I said, Mrs McCann's really nice. She's taken Tom and her wee boy Douglas to visit her sister, to let us get settled.'

Michael leant forward and breathed in. 'They're lovely. Really kind of her.'

She guided him across the corridor. 'This is us, here. Right opposite the table. The door's white.' She opened it. 'Our room.'

Having brought him in, she paused without meaning to
. . . was she expecting to hear him offer a polite remark about
how nice it *looked*? A split-second later, she added, 'I know
we'll be very happy here.'

'Thank you, Maggie. It feels fresh and inviting and . . .'

She closed the door behind them. 'We're home, Michael.'

They embraced and kissed. As he held her, she could feel
the handle of his stick press into her back.

She turned him towards the window. 'We've a really big
bay window. The park's just opposite. Grass that slopes all
the way up to Bruntsfield, there's paths for folk walking with
their kids. Lots of trees, too, really big some of them. Elms,
I think. Our curtains come down to the floor, they've got a
flower pattern on them, red and purple roses.' She guided him
a couple of steps. 'Here's your armchair . . . and here's mine.
They're light brown, high-backed and a bit old-fashioned
looking, but comfy enough. We'll sit in front of a gas fire
with a fine-looking wooden mantelpiece. It'll be cosy in the
evenings while Tom plays on the rug.' She took his hand again
and led him past the chairs and a small table. 'This . . . this
is our bed.'

Maggie had prepared a picnic for them to take across to the
park.

As she shook out the tartan blanket to let it settle flat on
the grass, she heard her mother's voice: *You've made your
bed, now you can lie on it.*

She shrugged and smiled to herself as she unpacked the
sandwiches wrapped in greaseproof paper – spam, mashed
egg – the thermos of tea, the cups and plates, some milk

in a brown medicine bottle, salt and pepper in little twists of paper. Laid out invitingly, the picnic meal looked good enough to be photographed for a magazine as a 'Family Day in the Park'. Yes, that's what it was, and what *they* were at last – a family. Maybe she'd write to her mother to let her know how well she was getting on, how happy she was. Maybe.

From then on, when she came up the front steps back from work, she'd see Michael standing at the window waiting for her. And every time, without thinking, she'd wave to him. Inside their room, she'd be greeted by his placing his hands on her face. That was the moment when she knew she was really home – the first of the perfect moments in the rest of her day. Next was Tom's excitement when she collected him from Mrs McCann. The third perfect moment happened several times: whenever she paused during the evening and allowed herself to feel their togetherness. The last was when she switched off the light and entered Michael's darkness.

A real family, yes – but they couldn't get married. Not yet – to do that would mean putting up banns in the name of Mr Stewart and Miss Davies, and the danger of making everything *public*. She felt like *Mrs Stewart*, she was known as *Mrs Stewart*. To everyone, apart from at Blair & Blair's, she *was* Mrs Stewart.

Tom had his first birthday: they shared their first Christmas together: then came Hogmanay – but not at Jean's. This time the New Year was seen in with Sheila and Gordon.

§

One freezing-cold day towards the end of January, Maggie was putting her key in the front door when—

'Oh, Miss Davies! Miss Davies! It's *you*, it's really *you*!'

Maggie turned to see the familiar tangle of blonde curls and smiling face. It was Donna.

SUNDAY AFTERNOON

Pull into the Rosehaven car park.

Taking your usual five in the contour leather to log on, to update.

Mandy.

Your agent.

Mandy again. Reliable girl.

GR8 CU@8 Tx

Two voice messages.

No hang-ups. Hang-ups are a message in themselves – if you're *not* there to answer, then you're not needed. Like you're a hang-up nearer to being dead.

But not you. Three texts. Two messages. Mr Magic lives!

Tweet the cottage get-out. Tweet another Sunday, another Mum visit.

Hoping it's a good day.

Psyched up, ready to rock'n'roll.

Once again you're standing on the yellow cross, your smile in place, flowers in one hand and the other raised in greeting for the CCTV. That's you on the screen – not looking so great. The loving son come to visit his elderly mother who's now seriously confused.

Yes, she's totally losing the place. She's like a book whose pages have fallen out of sequence – but who's going to put them back into their right order? There's no other copy to refer to.

Cue Mr Magic preparing to step onstage once more with his repertoire of well-tested tricks, his cheerful patter. Cue another Sunday. You'll make it a good one.

You're buzzed in. Heading straight down the corridor, on course to brighten up her—

Sudden swerve for the usual pit-stop in the visitors' WC. Dry heave and spit. And spit again. Take a few minutes to get focused, get upbeat.

Better?

You and your feelings back on track, you splash your face. The paper towel's screwed up and binned. You're ready to breeze through to the dayroom. You want to cheer her up. Be all sunshine and smiles.

The afternoon sun flooding the bay window with light, freeze-framing the scene: the high backed chairs, the foot-stools and zimmers, coffee tables, the TV, the Murray twins, sad Dorothy calling and calling . . .

But where's your mother?

Her chair's empty. Her zimmer's stainless steel tubing flashes its accusation: *You're late.*

Someone's taken her to the toilet?

But her zimmer's *here.* So how did she manage to—?

'Mr Stewart?' The young Polish girl's standing beside you. 'Mr Stewart? Please.'

Mariella? Marietta?

'You come, please.' She's not smiling.

Turning your back on the overheated hours burnt into the

dayroom walls, you follow Mariella / Marietta out into the hall. *Mariella.* Yes, that's her name.

She's wearing a green housecoat today, jeans and trainers. When she's signed up as your assistant you'll dress her in something special, something sleek, black and Futuristic. Distraction on high heels. It's the right time to upgrade. Invest in a new generation of high-tech props and—

'Room. Please, we go Mrs Stewart.'

'Mariella? Is my mother all right?'

The curtains have been pulled almost shut. A small lamp burns on the side table – its low watt glow washing over the room's stillness. You see your mother first in the dressing-table mirror and find yourself taking a half-step towards the reflected figure. Then immediately correct yourself.

Mariella's tilted the lampshade so the light falls more gently across your mother's face. A kindly girl . . . If she was dressed in sleek and shiny-black . . .

That time you watched her trying to get one of the Murray twins take her meds, you were shocked that the old woman could be so utterly unaware of the girl standing right in front of her, as if the Murray couldn't even *see* her. But what do *you* see now? Your ninety-year-old mother resting in her bed – do you really see *her*? Or is she becoming a fading memory already – the happiness in her voice whenever you phoned, her excited wave from the window as she saw you coming up the path?

'I go now.'

Don't go, Mariella, you want to say. *Please.*

At this moment you would give anything to be a genuine Mr Magic and make the glow return to her sunken cheeks, the glossy blackness to her hair, redness to her slack lips. No sleight of hand any more, no sleight of heart.

Not any longer.

Your mother's dying. You see it now. You're afraid you might burst into tears.

The chair beside her bed creaks as you sit down. It creaks again as you lean forward to take her hand.

Someone's just come into your room. You're aware of them sitting down in the chair beside your bed and can feel the warmth of their hand as it squeezes yours, the tenderness in their voice . . .

A farewell? The first of a hundred thousand welcomes?

Listen—

Within an hour of seeing Donna, the three of them had moved out of Glengyle Terrace. There was a family emergency, Maggie explained. Having thanked the McCanns for all their kindness, she promised she'd be in touch as soon as things settled. She didn't specify what things exactly. Her mother was mentioned. The rent was paid up for another fortnight, but Sheila should feel free to let the room from tomorrow.

One suitcase was all they took with them, and Michael's ex-army kitbag stuffed with Tom's clothes and bedding. What they couldn't carry, they left behind.

'Family emergency, right enough,' thought Maggie as she lifted their luggage into the taxi that would take them round to Jean's bakery. She was really sorry to be leaving Glengyle Terrace, but Mrs Saunders might appear at any moment, perhaps even bringing the police. Blair & Blair's, in turn, would probably be contacted. Maggie felt ashamed at lying to Sheila, but they couldn't risk staying even a day longer.

And so – no more Blair & Blair's and, most likely, no more Edinburgh.

What happened next was like a gift from heaven, a once-in-a-lifetime stroke of good luck. The advert in the *Scotsman* announced: 'Part-time home help wanted in exchange for rent-free cottage. Rural location. Apply in own handwriting.'

Maggie did, and received a reply by return, with a telephone number to phone. The cottage turned out to be the small gatehouse of an estate in the Borders. Learning that her husband was a veteran who'd been blinded in the war, the laird clearly took pity on them. Maggie said they could come immediately.

There's the sound of doors opening and closing, the tap of someone's walking stick on the linoleum out in the corridor, a woman saying she hopes there might be some cake.

Your familiar room. Your wardrobe. Armchair. Wash hand basin and mirror. Tea trolley with playing cards laid out for the game of patience you will probably never finish—

A fortnight after they'd moved in, Maggie was seated at her small work table in the living room, grinning with pleasure as she inserted the first sheet of foolscap into her typewriter.

No wonder she was grinning – on learning that his new help could not only type but knew how to keep basic accounts, the laird had at once offered her the position of part-time secretary to the factor of his estate. And so – no more mops and pails, brushes and carpet beaters, no more dripping, heavy-wet bedsheets needing hung out and then ironed. If she wanted, she was even allowed to take in extra typing work from the village to do in her own time. Michael had soon learned his way about the cottage and within a few days was walking up to the big house and round the grounds all by himself.

Maggie glanced over the top of her typewriter – there had been a real blizzard during the night and now a blue-skied, snow-silenced winter's day waited for her outside. The fields and hedgerows were white, the telegraph poles and their wires stretched in a line like so many pencil marks pointing out a hidden road to the village. Once she'd finished typing up Rev McKay's service for the following morning, the three of them would wrap up well and go for a walk down by the river, now surely frozen over.

Winter gave way to spring. Mrs Stewart wrote regularly to Michael, far too regularly. The news and gossip from Stornoway always came heavily larded with complaints and veiled accusations – her bad back made running the lodging house more and more difficult, the struggle to live on her war widow's pension was getting harder and harder. She missed her son and needed him, needed him desperately.

Michael would listen in grim silence, then apologise to Maggie saying his mother couldn't help herself, she was angry, that was all. Give her a while longer to accept things. Once they'd got married, which they'd do in secret, he'd ask if they could come and visit. It would mean waiting until the moment was right, of course . . .

By this time Maggie would have put the hateful letter back in its envelope and stuck it in the drawer with the others. The letters made her furious – the venom in the old woman's words was really directed at her. Not that she was ever mentioned, or Tom. It was like they didn't exist. Very soon she began to edit as she read. Maggie always typed the replies which Michael then took to the village post office next time he was doing the shopping.

On a May morning about four months after they'd moved in, there was a rap on the cottage door. Norman the Post. Michael was making a pot of tea. Having been to answer, Maggie returned to the living room:

'A letter. Don't know the handwriting.'

Struggling to push aside the duvet – as if you could somehow manage to get young Maggie's attention. You want to comfort her. You want to grab at the letter she's about to read, to snatch it out of her hand.

But then what?

You know what's going to happen. You can't stop it now, any more than you could have stopped it back then. You can do nothing but watch.

Carefully as always, Michael places a plate of biscuits on the tea-trolley. 'Postmark?' he asks.

Postmark. She ought to have checked first, before saying anything. But it's too late now.

'Stornoway.'

'It's from Lachlan – not heard from him in ages.'

But she knows it's not from Lachlan. She knows Lachlan's

handwriting – all those letters from Michael she's kept in her treasure box.

You watch her pick up the letter knife. Watch her slit open the envelope.

Were this a kinder world, Maggie would sense you beside her as she reads out the letter from Mrs Stewart's neighbour:

Dear Michael, I'm sorry to have to write to you with bad news but . . .

Michael's mother had slipped in the street – it was a serious fall. She'd needed an ambulance. She was back home now and holding her own, so far. Could Michael come as soon as possible?

The soothing warmth of someone's hand as they continue to sit here holding yours. No need to say anything, no need to make the effort to open your eyes—

Maggie's spoken to the guard who helped her put Michael onto the train at Lockerbie station. Lockerbie, Carstairs, Glasgow Central and then the West Highland Line to Mallaig, the ferry across to Lewis – he'll be passed from guard to guard like a precious parcel to be delivered safely to his mother in Stornoway.

You are with Maggie now on the platform, giving her the courage she needs to send the man she loves on his way. Giving her the courage to kiss him goodbye.

Together you share the warmth of his fingertips as they pass over her eyes, her cheeks, her lips: 'So's I'll have something to remember you,' he whispers.

There's a belch-belch-belch of grey smoke as the engine shudders forward, its wheels gaining traction on the steel rails. Straining, it gradually picks up speed and pulls out of the station. When the train has disappeared from sight, you accompany Maggie and Tom back towards the exit, ready to return with them to the gatehouse, ready to help them through the coming days, weeks, months.

No longer having the strength to hold on, drifting to and fro, from moment to moment—

Once again you are back with young Maggie Davies on her ferry trip across to Stornoway, once again you can feel the salt dampness soaking into your coat and scarf, its freshness tightening the skin on your face.

The handrail is ice-cold. Slate-coloured waves slide over each other, sealing in a stretch of water whose briefly churned-up surface always flattens afterwards to a dead calm. The small boat trails silence in its wake. Together you look down into the depths, and shudder with an abruptness that makes the blood stall in your heart, the breath catch in your throat . . .

Your body trembles; your nerves seize. Held under the weight of the duvet, your arm again struggles to raise itself as though to grasp hold of an invisible clock's next tick and force it on—

It is late September, a glorious autumn morning. The post has just been and you've returned indoors with another of Michael's weekly letters. You expect it will be filled with the usual words of love and reassurance, the usual hopes and promises. He's been away for nearly five months.

You sit down at your work table, slit open the envelope.

The doctor, he writes, now believes that though she will likely live for a good many years to come, his mother will never regain her full strength and mobility. It seems that she'll always need someone to look after her. She has never left the island and now she never will.

I'm all she's got, he explains, *and so I'll have to stay here with*—

You let the page drop. You know what's coming. With every passing week, you'd grown to dread Norman the Post's rap at the door. You'd been half-expecting this letter, but now that it's arrived, it's almost a relief. You glance over at Tom who's sitting on the floor next to the tea-trolley, completely absorbed in throwing your playing cards around the room. Seeing you look at him, he holds out a crushed fistful towards you.

Michael goes on to say that he loves you and misses you. He misses you more and more each day. He misses Tom, too.

And *you* miss him. You love him and know he will be the only man in your life. But what did Mrs Saunders say that time – *love is the easy bit*?

When the time is right, he continues, he'll start telling his mother about their plans to get married. So far it's not been possible to say anything . . . she's very easily upset . . . but as soon as there's an opportunity . . . pick his moment carefully . . . take time . . . he's sure you understand . . . talk her into allowing you and Tom . . . because he can't leave her, not now she . . .

Having folded up the letter, you put it back into its

envelope, place it on the table. For several minutes you sit with your hands in your lap, head bowed, staring down at your neatly written name and address, and at the slightly smudged Stornoway postmark . . .

Letting your breathing ease back to normal, your heartbeat steady itself once more—

You're feeling very tired suddenly. A very pleasant tiredness, as though you were already half-asleep—

An hour later you've written your reply, sealed the envelope and stamped it. If you leave now, you will be in time to catch the post. The sooner the letter goes, the better.

You lift Tom into his pushchair, put on your coat, your hat.

Last thing, you glance in the hall mirror to check your appearance. A dab of powder, a quick touch of lipstick.

You're ready.

The buttons of your coat fastened up and your hat straightened, you give yourself a smile. You've written to Michael for the last time. You've dried your tears. You have made your decision and will stick to it. You will manage, somehow. The door pulled shut, you start off down the front path.

A gust of wind sets the fallen leaves swirling around your feet, and when you scoop up a handful to scatter over his head Tom tries grabbing them as they tumble all about him. He's laughing and squealing.

'WHEE!' You send him and his pushchair several yards ahead of you along the road. A few steps and you catch up. 'WHEE . . .!' Pushing him again several yards ahead. Then hurrying after him to catch up. Above, the sky is a clear and cloudless blue. Small birds flit in and out of the hedgerows on either side and it feels like they're keeping you—

ACKNOWLEDGEMENTS

Excerpts of this novel have appeared in the *Scotsman* and *Gutter 09*. The author would like to gratefully acknowledge a Royal Literature Fund Fellowship at Edinburgh University (Office of Lifelong Learning), which allowed him time to write. Grateful thanks also to my wonderful editor Nick Royle, to my ultra-patient agent Lucy Luck, to Lesley Glaister, Andrew Greig, Moez Surani and Dora Staub for their valuable comments, and most of all to my wife Regi Claire for her insightful readings of the text through its many versions, and for her endless patience and support. This novel was written while I was the Edinburgh Makar / Poet Laureate and I would like to thank the City of Edinburgh Council and the Edinburgh UNESCO City of Literature for their support during this period, in particular Lynne Halfpenny, Denise Brace, Ali Bowden, Peggy Hughes and Sarah Morrison.